STEVE HEUZINKVELD

SCAVENGERS OF THE FALL

THE FALL SERIES BOOK THREE

First edition

ISBN: 978-0-6452886-5-0

This book was professionally typeset on Reedsy.
Find out more at reedsy.com

Dedicated to my son, Jacob.
Hopefully, you'll be 18 when you read this.

Foreword

While this story is based on real locations throughout the United States, I have used fictitious names for some towns and neighborhoods, so that I can change certain aspects of these locations for the sake of the story.

Thank you, and enjoy!

CHAPTER 1

"You're not gonna find something like this for a while," Keith Bowman grunted, dropping the dead woman's corpse onto the living room's carpet.

"Yeah, looks like you lucked out," Sterling Granger agreed, swinging another stiff up onto the couch. "Anything worth finding now is either buried or carried."

"I know, it just feels so tacky," Riley Armstrong replied as she drew weathered curtains across the room's broken window, giving them cover from the street.

She knew that the sight of the damp dirty canvas would only be announcing their presence in the bleak suburban neighborhood, but she figured that whoever had left the pair of bodies out on the road would have already noticed that something was amiss.

"Don't tell me you're getting squeamish over a dead give-away," Keith shot her a grin as he wrangled the backpack off the woman's corpse.

"*Dead giveaway*," Sterling echoed with a dry chuckle as he patted the pockets of the man with a hole in his chest. "Good one."

"Looting a corpse is one thing, but wearing its shoes…" Riley trailed off as she sank down to her knees anyway, pulling her gloves off before untying the dead woman's boots.

"Where do you think organ donations used to come from?" Keith asked rhetorically as he rummaged through the backpack, his grin souring as he fished out a smashed jar of preserves. He tossed the slimy shards aside before nodding at the pair of boots. "If it makes you feel any better, they can't smell any shittier than we do."

The first boot came off with a stubborn *thock*.

He was right.

If there was a stench coming from the cadaver's feet, it wasn't registering for Riley.

They had been living on the road for months, using whatever water they could find to drink rather than for showering.

The last time she had felt reasonably clean was a few weeks ago, after a quick plunge into a cold river. She had regretted it from the moment that she had resurfaced, the wintry wind reducing her to a bundle of shivering skin and bones until she got dressed again.

"Don't think about it – just put them on," Sterling looked up at her as he laid out his loot on the coffee table. "Your sneakers aren't gonna do you any good when winter really hits."

Riley bit her bottom lip as she examined the dead woman's shoes.

They were strong and sturdy, probably meant for hiking.

There was no doubt that they could survive slogging through the snowy weather.

And best of all, they were her size.

Holding the pair of boots upside down, she knocked them together a few times, half-expecting a clump of crawling maggots to fall out.

Nothing.

She breathed a small sigh of relief before summoning her resolve, kicking off her sneakers and slipping on the second-hand shoes.

"Congratulations," Keith gave her two mocking claps of applause. "I'd hate to see you shopping though. You only had one option and you still took your sweet ass time."

"Fuck you," Riley gave him a small snort, lacing up her new boots as she nodded at the backpack. "You find anything?"

"Half-empty packet of crackers," Keith stood up and kicked the bag over. "Can't eat it though. Not unless you want a blood-coated cracker sandwich." He looked over at Sterling. "What about you?"

"Bunch of lock picks and a switchblade," Sterling reported, sitting back in an armchair to preside over his pitiful prize.

"We can't go back empty-handed," Riley reminded them both, pushing her empty stomach to the back of her mind. "Not again."

Keith nodded in somber acknowledgment before sidling over to the window, fingering the weathered curtain aside and peering out at the street.

The former police officer had lost his beefy physique, his big cords of muscle having shrunken to ropey dense remnants after the series of long stretches in between their meager meals. He still filled out Nolan Armstrong's fur-lined leather aviator jacket, but only because it had been too tight for Keith to begin with.

Similarly, Sterling had turned from lean to gaunt, the ex-rancher now casting a stark figure in the loose folds of his green parka and camouflage trousers.

Even Riley had lost her slender frame – the only curve that she had left underneath her gray hoodie and jeans was her bloated belly.

A small part of her began to envy the pair of corpses in the living room. Their deaths must have felt like a sweet release, compared to the struggle of surviving on the edge of starvation each and every dreary desolate day.

"Something doesn't add up," she pulled her gloves back on as a thought occurred to her. "These two shouldn't have had *anything* on them. Who the hell's going around shooting people and not even stopping to at least check their backpacks?"

"Somebody who doesn't need to," Sterling shrugged, before tilting his head at the idea. "Maybe whoever killed these guys aren't that desperate."

"Or maybe they're just trying to protect what they've got," Keith stepped away from the window, looking at them both with renewed vigor in his stony gaze. "There's a stash in the house across the street."

"How do you know?" Riley asked, rising to her feet to peer between the damp curtains.

A brisk wind greeted her as it blew through the broken window, swirling frosty air across her face.

She didn't even know which house he was talking about.

They all looked exactly the same.

On the other side of the road was a row of identical double-story weatherboard homes, each one either lined with barren trees and bushes or leaning chain-linked fences.

This neighborhood looks like it was abandoned a long time ago, she thought to herself.

Windswept piles of broken glass twinkled in the pale winter

sun.

Overgrown stalks of dead grass stood stubbornly over the dusting of snow.

Tags of graffiti decorated most of the forgotten houses and cars – a parting gift from the first few waves of scavengers who had picked the homes clean.

A breath of winter blew again, wind whistling through the boarded-up windows of one double-story house across the street.

Riley furrowed her eyebrows as she glanced sidelong at Keith.

"You don't barricade an abandoned house," he finished her thought as he drew his pistol.

CHAPTER 2

"How do you wanna do this?" Riley Armstrong cupped her gloved hands together and blew, warm breath misting back up into her face.

"Same way we did last time," Keith Bowman replied, counting the bullets in his pistol's magazine before ramming it home and thumbing the slide release.

"Last time?" Sterling Granger echoed as he surveyed the street.

Riley and Keith had agreed to keep the story between themselves.

They hadn't wanted anyone else judging them.

She was afraid of what their group might think if she told them that they had raided an old man's cellar, taking half of his food and supplies that he had gathered up to endure the approaching winter.

Sometimes she would lose sleep over it, thinking about how immoral they had become – stealing to survive, regardless of whoever had to pay the price.

But on those long cold nights, when she lay awake with an empty stomach growling at her in the darkness, she silently wished that they had taken more.

"Are you sure?" Riley studied the resolved expression on Keith's face as she unshouldered her backpack. She jerked her head towards the pair of dead bodies in the living room, both of them grim reminders of the consequences if things went awry. "I mean, look how far they got."

"Worked out for us last time," Keith shrugged, stroking his stubbled jaw.

Riley rubbed the back of her neck, hesitation written plainly across her face as she stared back at him.

Taking a deep breath, she knelt down on the carpet to rummage through the few contents of her backpack, seizing hold of an empty glass bottle.

"Remember – don't shoot unless we have to," Keith added, lifting one side of his fur-lined leather aviator jacket to holster his pistol again.

"Wait, we're not using the guns?" Sterling let the weathered curtains fall back into place as he turned away from the window. "Fuck that. If you don't want it, give it to me. I'm not dying today, and it's been too long since any of us have eaten."

"They're still people – innocent people," the former police officer growled, squaring up, his jaw set with stubborn determination. "Killing them is easy. What comes after isn't. Trust me."

"Everyone's desperate," Riley shouldered her backpack again as she rose to her feet. She looked into Sterling's dark eyes, "But we're not there yet."

As much as she wanted to agree with the ex-rancher, she had to side with Keith, if only for the sake of her own conscience.

Keith gave her a nod of approval as he took the empty glass bottle from her, proud that she still knew where to draw the line between right and wrong, however thin that line had become.

"Well, we might not be there yet," Sterling's lips twisted skeptically as he glanced over at the dead man's corpse on the couch. "But I have a damn strong feeling we're about to be."

Leaving the pair of bodies in the living room, Keith led the way through to the back of the house, climbing over an overturned fridge and navigating past windswept debris into the snow-dusted backyard.

"Follow Riley's lead and wait for my signal," he instructed Sterling, before his stony gaze went to Riley.

He didn't need to say *be careful*.

She already knew.

The moment passed, and they took off in opposite directions, staying low as they stole into the neighbor's yard.

"Keep up and stay quiet," Riley whispered over her shoulder as she caught a glimpse of the double-story house with its boarded-up windows.

A chain-linked fence gave a slight jingle as they jumped behind another abandoned home, the barrel of her pistol pressing into the small of her back.

Flitting between barren trees and bushes, they snuck through six more backyards, just to be certain that they wouldn't be spotted by the shooter when they crossed the street.

She crouched beside the corner of a wooden veranda, shallow puffs of mist escaping her lips as she steadied her breathing.

Sterling crept up behind her, keeping his head below the level of the veranda's deck as he pulled back the hood of his parka.

8

"How do we know they don't have lookouts posted any-where else?" he whispered, checking over his shoulder.

"We don't," Riley realized as she scoped out the barricaded house again.

In the corner of her eye, Keith dashed across the street farther down the road.

There was no time to reconsider the plan.

CHAPTER 3

"Come on," Riley Armstrong urged as she crawled out from behind the wooden veranda, using a snow-choked flowerbed for cover as she stealthily advanced towards the street.

Sterling Granger followed on his elbows and knees until they reached the edge of the frosty overgrown lawn.

Snapping up into a run towards the opposite row of houses, Riley was grateful for the spiky grooves of her new shoes, the dead woman's hiking boots crunching over the powdered asphalt with ease.

Her old sneakers would have slipped on the street's snowy surface well before they could skitter over to the other side.

A nasty stench pervaded their nostrils as they approached the passage between a pair of paint-peeling weatherboard homes.

Two overturned trash cans that had been fermenting since the advent of the apocalypse lay uncovered in the walkway, rifled through by the local wildlife – sometime before the reek had become strong enough to snuff out a small animal.

"This way," Riley almost gagged on her own words, turning to climb into one of the houses through an open window, her gloved hands brushing over broken glass.

A rash of gooseflesh flowered down her arms as she eased herself inside.

Something bad had happened here.

She could feel it.

Shelves of stuffed bears glared at the pair of intruders, while a half-assembled crib cowered in the corner, with a handful of screws scattered around forgotten wooden pieces on the floor.

Driven onward by the putrid smell of the festering garbage outside, Riley and Sterling pressed through the nursery, wisps of dust swirling around their feet as the empty house shivered with a series of ghostly creaks.

The slight sounds of their shoes scuffing the floorboards were magnified in the stillness, while the doors of a dark linen closet held its breath as they passed by.

Shadows seemed to leap out at them from behind drab dingy furniture, with every surface mottled in mournful gray.

Even the house across the street – with two dead bodies lying in the living room – had felt livelier than this place.

All too happy to leave, Riley's relief to see the broken back windows was short-lived, as a new stench assaulted her senses.

The reek of rotting cabbage mixed with moldy garlic emanated from the kitchen.

Sticking out from behind the raided pantry's open door, the crisp orange cloth of a flowery summer dress lay marred in a tarry pool of sludge. Decaying fingers clutched the handle of a kitchen knife, the keen edge of its dull blade unstained, the woman's weapon either too short or too slow to put up a fight against whoever had broken in.

Neither Riley nor Sterling had the stomach to venture any

closer – not even for the possibility that there might still be some baby formula inside the pantry.

Some things were better left unseen.

They ducked out through one of the broken back windows, climbing down into the yard without a backwards glance.

Riley gasped a lungful of frigid fresh air, silently wishing that they had chosen a different route.

They crept through tufts of snowy overgrown grass, padding past rusty sheds and swing sets, derelict dog kennels and tree houses, until they caught sight of Keith Bowman hunkered down in the distance.

He was crouched beside a brick barbecue pit in the backyard neighboring the house with the boarded-up windows. Still clutching the empty glass bottle, he watched them approach from the other side, jerking his head up with a slight frown, as if to ask, *what took you so long?* Or, more likely, *where's yours?*

Riley stopped short of the last house beside their target, using the building for cover as she shrugged off her backpack.

Peering inside the bag, she fished out a coiled length of wire that had once been a coat hanger. Straightening out the wire, she shouldered her backpack again and flashed Keith a thumbs-up.

He nodded his acknowledgment before slowly poking his head out from behind the brick barbecue pit, checking the barricaded double-story home. Seeing that the coast was clear, he waved his free hand towards the front.

Still using the last neighboring house for cover, Riley and Sterling crept along the side towards the street, dropping to their stomachs as they cleared the corner.

Hearts thumping in their chests, they crawled across the neighbor's driveway and pawed through the brush of the untended front yard like a pair of wildcats stalking their prey, the house with the boarded-up windows looming larger with every inch forward.

Shit – fucking idiot, Riley cursed herself the moment she saw the driveway on the far side of the barricaded house.

Somewhere in between debating about the guns and splitting up, they had gotten their angles of approach mixed up.

With the snow-dusted street a no-man's land, every treacherous foot forward seemed like a mile, and Riley and Sterling still had a whole lot more distance to travel, not to mention the chain-linked fence in between.

They had to double-back to Keith, before –

CRASH!

The glass bottle smashed somewhere out back, deafening in the silence.

"What the hell was that?" a whispered shout rose up from behind the barricaded windows, "Are they back already?"

"Can't be," a second voice replied from the upper level, huskier than the first. "Fuck! Those two we wasted are gone."

"Bullshit, they were still there last time I checked," the first one whispered back. "Pretty sure I nailed them both in the chest."

"Pretty sure you missed," the second voice scolded. "Keep watching the street, I'll check the back. Fucking hell, Taylor…"

Riley glanced over her shoulder at Sterling as a pair of footfalls scuttled downstairs and faded towards the back of the house.

For a moment, she considered dropping the length of wire and reaching for her pistol.

It would have been all too easy to blast a few well-placed bullets in through the house's boarded-up windows.

Then they wouldn't have to settle for only half the food – they could take it all.

She wondered whether another scavenger had similar thoughts a few months ago, back when a pregnant woman had been caught off guard wearing her orange summer dress, and only a kitchen knife to defend herself with.

Sticking to the plan, Riley stole across the snow-dusted grass towards the chain-linked fence, glimpsing a rifle's muzzle poking out between the front room's two planks of wood.

The weapon was pointing out towards the street.

Thankfully, whoever was inside hadn't noticed the pair of figures creeping closer from their neighbor's front yard.

Riley's pupils dilated as she frantically watched the rifle's barrel swaying to and fro.

Palms sweating inside her gloves, she clenched the old coat hanger's length of wire in between her teeth.

Using both hands to hold the chain-linked fence's railing, she jumped over the barrier in one smooth leap, landing softly on the snowy grass on the other side.

She quickly ducked down underneath the level of the front room's windowsill as Sterling followed her lead.

Removing the wire from her mouth, Riley began crawling along the front of the house towards the driveway, when a metallic jingle rang out behind her.

Heart in her throat, she whipped her head around.

The loose folds of Sterling's green parka had snagged on the fence.

CHAPTER 4

Sterling Granger was lying flat on the ground, struggling with the hem of his green parka caught on the chain-linked fence.

GUVV!!

The hunting rifle woofed a finger of hot lead, ripping a hole through his jacket.

Riley Armstrong scrambled underneath the front room's boarded-up window, her anxious gaze trained on the gun's barrel as it jerked to reload another round into the chamber.

"Heather?" a jittery girl's voice from behind the window called. "I think I've got something out here!"

"Handle it, Taylor!" Heather yelled back from the other end of the house. "There's someone in the neighbor's yard."

Cracks of gunfire rang out through the air.

Unable to free himself from the snag, Sterling unzipped his jacket and shrugged himself out of it, leaving his backpack behind underneath the garment.

He threw his back against the front of the house as a rustle sounded from within, the shooter adjusting her footing to probe the ground with her hunting rifle.

Heart hammering in her chest, Riley signaled to Sterling to

cover up the shallow breaths misting from his mouth.

Hyperventilating, mere inches from death, he drew the collar of his gray undershirt up over the lower half of his face, staring up in wide-eyed horror as the rifle's steaming muzzle traced ever closer to his skull.

Riley flexed her gloved fingers, eyes focused on the rifle.

The length of the barrel protruding from the front room's window was too short.

There was no way that Riley could grab it without getting her fingers blown off.

Glancing back at Sterling, she lifted her hips up off the ground, swift but silent, reaching for the pistol tucked into the waistband of her jeans at the small of her back.

"Fucking wind," Taylor huffed, muttering to herself as the barrel of her hunting rifle swept back out towards the street again. "How you doing back there, Heather?"

"I'd be doing a whole lot better if you shut the hell up!" Heather shouted her reply, her husky voice taut with tension. She yelled out a warning to anyone listening, "Whoever's fucking with us, you better hope my aim's improved. Last guy I shot ended up killing himself after I blew his nuts off!"

Riley stifled a smirk.

She liked these girls.

But that wasn't going to fill her empty stomach.

Easing her hand off the hilt of her pistol, she gestured to Sterling to take her position underneath the windowsill.

There was still a chance that they could disarm the shooters without a standoff.

Still clutching the former coat hanger's length of wire, Riley soundlessly skulked along the front of the house, pinpointing a quiet path through the snowy grass with feline precision.

Like a prowling panther, she pawed up onto the narrow porch's concrete slab, gently lowering herself down on the other side.

Finally reaching the driveway, she breathed a sigh of relief as she reared up alongside the garage's roller door. Now that she was outside the field of view from the front room's window, as well as the boarded-up lookout spots upstairs, it was time to go to work.

Standing slightly off-center to the garage, she slowly fed the length of wire's hooked end in between the top of the roller door and the rubber weather seal lining the entrance.

During all of Keith's years on the force working alongside Nolan Armstrong, the veteran police officer had picked up a thing or two from the felons that they had apprehended. And now, since breaking and entering into properties had become a necessary skill for survival, he had passed on that criminal knowledge to Riley.

Having cast her fishing line, Riley pivoted the length of wire towards the center of the garage's roller door, mentally picturing the emergency release handle dangling down. After months of practice, she could feel the slight shift in resistance as she hooked the cord, and she gently pulled back the wire, until she heard a *click* resounding from within.

Coiling up the length of wire and silently stowing it away into her backpack, she glanced over her shoulder at Sterling, who was still lying in wait underneath the boarded-up window.

With him and Keith already in position, Riley knew that it was on her to make the next move.

Squatting down on her haunches, she curled her gloved fingertips around one of the roller door's grooves, when a familiar shiver shuddered up her spine.

All I wanted to do... was help people, Alyssa Quinn's final words of madness echoed eerily, the cultist doctor's bulging purple face swimming in Riley's vision as she struggled for air, her windpipe crushed underneath the weight of her own lodge's garage door.

Riley shook herself back to the present, and in one fluid motion, she threw the roller door open with a metallic screech.

Dropping flat onto the driveway, with one hand on the hilt of her pistol, Riley scanned the garage for any signs of life.

Besides a faded yellow hatchback, a workbench stocked with dusty tools, and an old pair of cracked brown leather couches, the garage was empty.

"Heather!" Taylor's panicked scream came from behind the front room's boarded-up window, "They're coming in through the garage!!"

The shooter leaned out to see if she could get a clear shot at the intruders, when Sterling reached up and seized the rifle's barrel, a stray round going off as he yanked the firearm out between the planks of wood, hot lead punching into the grass.

"SHIT!" Sterling threw one arm over his head as he scrambled towards the porch.

BADOOM!!

Wood splinters exploded as a shotgun blast snapped at his heels, kicking up a clump of turf and snow.

"Motherfucker!!" Taylor shouted as she cocked another shell into the breech of her backup weapon. "Get the fuck away from our house!!"

"It's us or them!" Sterling's dark eyes met Riley's as he took cover behind the porch's concrete slab, propping up the rifle to draw a bead on the silhouette in the window. "I told you before, I'm not dying today."

"Not yet," Riley held up a pacifying hand, pleading him for more time. "We're not there yet."

"We're pretty fucking close!" he barked, balling up behind the concrete slab as another shotgun blast peppered the porch.

"Hold them off!" Heather shouted from the other end of the house, "I'm on my way!"

Icy adrenaline pumping through her veins, Riley dashed across the length of the garage, throwing her back against the rear corner just as the side door's handle began to turn.

Small puffs of mist escaped her lips, floating in the frigid air for what felt like an eternity.

Three blind slugs punched through the wooden door, one bullet biting off the drawstring of Riley's gray hoodie.

The door flung open, and a pistol swung out into the garage.

Riley's boot rose and thrust, stomping the door shut on the shooter's wrist, drawing a high-pitched scream of agony as the gun clattered to the floor.

Surging out of the corner, Riley latched onto the writhing hand and *pulled*, using all that remained of her bodyweight to drag the shooter through the doorway, sending her sprawling over the faded yellow hatchback's hood.

"Heather!?" Taylor's quavering voice called from the front room, "Hang tight, I'm coming!"

"Not if you want her to live!" Riley slammed the side door shut and picked up the dropped handgun, keeping a wary eye on Heather. Not taking any chances, she lined up the pistol's sights, "Any sudden moves and you're both dead."

"You call that a threat, bitch?" Heather rolled off the hatchback's hood, cradling her swollen wrist as she slumped down onto the garage floor.

She was a redhead, and looked to be either in her late teens or her early forties.

It was the same for Riley.

The apocalypse had aged everyone prematurely, and nobody had any reason to cling onto a number anymore.

"No, that's a promise," Riley's grip on the pistol shook with adrenaline, but from this distance, she could put a bullet right between her eyes, or near enough to make no difference.

"A quick death's all anyone can hope for these days," Heather shrugged in nonchalance. A shadow crossed her face as she glowered up at Riley. "But if you touch my sister, I swear, I'll come back to haunt you. I will manifest in the back of your eyelids. I'm not kidding – I'll make you see some nasty shit. You won't be able to eat. You won't be able to sleep. I'll break you down until you're so weak, my ghost will fucking *possess* you… and then I'll really start having some fun."

Damn, I need to work on my threats, Riley thought to herself.

"What are you waiting for?" Heather challenged, staring down the barrel of her own gun with indifference. "Pull the trigger, see what happens."

"You think I don't already see the people I've killed?" Riley gave her a small snort, cycling through all of the dead faces even as she held the girl at gunpoint. But those people had deserved to die. This one didn't. "You know, there's still a way that you and your sister can survive this."

"There sure is," Heather agreed, craning her neck around the front of the faded yellow hatchback to stare out at the snow-dusted street. "Looks like you're in for a real treat."

Riley wasn't buying it.

But in the corner of her eye, she caught the garage's side door softly swinging open, and the barrel of a shotgun nosed out beside her.

CHAPTER 5

"You take that gun off my sister," a freckled red-haired girl with braces warned, "Or I'll blow a hole through your stomach so big, I could wear your waist like a fucking sleeve."

"Nice one, Taylor," Heather smiled, rising to her feet. She held her good hand out to Riley, glancing pointedly at the pistol, "I'll have that back now. Thanks for keeping it warm for me."

Riley's chest deflated, and she held up her hands, pointing the gun at the ceiling.

She wanted to avoid giving the freckled girl any reason for getting an itchy trigger finger.

"You might wanna rethink about where you're aiming that shotgun," Riley spoke over her shoulder to the smaller sister as she calmly paced over to the rear wall of the garage, turning back around to face them both.

"Why's that?" Taylor asked, stepping into the garage with a mixture of triumph and curiosity on her face.

"Hey, the gun, remember?" Heather demanded, her hand still outstretched.

"Because I didn't come alone," Riley ignored her, holding the freckled girl's gaze as she nodded towards the snow-powdered street.

"Oh, nice try," Taylor scoffed, sharing a knowing smirk with her sister. "I just nailed your friend in the fucking face. Don't try to use our own tricks on us."

"This friend?" Sterling Granger's gaunt face appeared beside the garage's entrance, the hunting rifle's stock in his shoulder as he held the girl at gunpoint.

Taylor swung her shotgun towards him, when another pistol emerged from the side door, the barrel nestling in her red hair.

"Think real hard, kid," Keith Bowman's whiskey-cured voice warned. "You only got one shot. We got plenty."

Just to throw more weight to his words, Riley whipped out her other pistol, one for each of the two sisters, holding them both at her mercy.

"What do I do?" the girl's voice cracked as she glanced towards her big sister.

"Fucking hell, Taylor!" Heather fumed, her veil of nonchalance vanishing from her face. "Put the gun down, before you get three more holes in your head!"

Crestfallen, Taylor gingerly set the shotgun down on the garage floor before shuffling over towards Heather, unable to look at her in the eye.

"I'm gonna go clear the rest of the house," Keith declared, checking over his shoulder. Before leaving though, he lingered in the doorway for a moment, "Riley, remember to watch your back while there's still an active shooter hanging around. That's how this two-bit chickenshit shrimp-witted imp-chick got the drop on you."

"That's why I brought you along," Riley sassed him out of the side of her mouth.

Holding both sisters at gunpoint, she jerked her head towards one of the cracked brown leather couches.

"Looks like we're getting robbed by the rhyming raiders," Heather supposed as Keith shut the side door behind him.

"That was him being polite," Sterling strode into the garage, stopping the pair of sisters before he tore the couch's cushions out, making sure that there were no hidden surprises underneath. He nodded towards Taylor, "If I had to name you, I'd call you a red-haired yellow-bellied shit-stained runt."

"Calm down, Camo Pants," Taylor teased him as she flopped down onto the couch's base beside her sister. "You're in my house now. You learn some respect."

Riley found herself having to stifle another smirk as Heather cracked up laughing.

"You..." Sterling reached over his shoulder to adjust his parka's hood, before realizing that his jacket was still hanging on the fence outside. Exhaling his frustration, he marched over to the garage's workbench, finding a roll of duct tape among the dusty array of tools. Propping the hunting rifle up against the table, he returned to the couch, "You almost shot me four times, and you put a hole through my jacket. I'll call you whatever the hell I damn well please."

"It was his favorite jacket," Riley explained, trying her best to keep everyone calm, even as Sterling began binding their hands together with tape. "You'd think we would've found something else by now, but..." She glanced down at her own clothes – the same ones that she had been wearing ever since the morning Grandma Eleanor had died. "My dad got me this hoodie when I said I was cold at the mall. It's the last thing I have left of him now."

She had no idea why she was sharing her story with a couple

of complete strangers who had been shooting at them only a few minutes ago.

But she wanted them to know that she wasn't just some soulless raider who got a kick out of slinging threats and stealing supplies.

She and her group were still human beings, who had lived happy normal lives once, before all this – before survival had become more important than civilization.

"We lost our dad too," Heather turned around to see Riley's pistols still pointed at the backs of their heads, and her sympathetic face instantly hardened. "But do you see either of us going around rob– ah, FUCK!"

She jerked her hands away from Sterling's duct tape, cradling her swollen wrist.

"That's what you get for saying Dad's gone," Taylor bristled beside her.

"It's been *months*, Taylor," she reminded her sister, who didn't want to hear it.

"Tie her arms to her thighs," Riley nodded at Sterling as she lowered the pair of guns. It had all been for show anyway. The last thing she wanted to do was kill two innocent girls who were just trying to get by on their own. "Heather, for what it's worth, I'm sorry about your wrist. You know, if we hadn't been on the edge of starving for the past three months, one of your bullets might have actually done some damage."

"Is that supposed to make me feel better?" Heather wondered, eyeing Sterling as he wrapped her up with what was left of the duct tape. "Or is that just one of the many benefits of starving that we'll have to look forward to?"

"The first few weeks are the hardest," Sterling finished binding her up, tossing aside the empty roll of tape as he rose to his feet. "After that, you get used to it."

"Yeah?" Taylor raised her eyebrows, struggling against her restraints now that he couldn't replace them. "Well, I hope you enjoy your last meal then, fucker, because when our friends get back –"

"Shut up," Heather hushed her, unable to do anything else other than hunch over her bound arms. "Dad's gone. Our friends are gone. It's just the two of us now."

"Oh, nice try," Riley narrowed her eyes at the pair of sisters, stepping out from behind the couch to scan the snow-dusted street for any signs of movement.

Sterling picked up the hunting rifle again, crouching beside the garage's entrance to check their flanks.

Seeing nothing, Riley turned back to the two girls before they got any other ideas.

"You're the lookouts for a bigger group," she surmised, watching Taylor's scowl drop a hint of alarm. "You got lucky today. We didn't come here to hurt anyone. But if you come after us, you'll only get yourselves and your friends killed. And then we'll have to come back here for the rest of the shit that you should've been happy with."

"You're not taking it all?" Heather asked, unsure of whether she had heard her correctly.

"Everybody has to eat," Riley shrugged, despite her empty stomach's protests against settling for only half the haul.

"So, you're *not* with the tour bus?" Taylor frowned, glancing sidelong at her sister.

"Tour bus?" Sterling echoed in confusion.

Before they could press any further, the side door opened, and Keith stepped back into the garage.

"House is clear," he reported, before locking eyes with Riley,

26

"This is the one we've been waiting for."

CHAPTER 6

Riley Armstrong's backpack hadn't felt this heavy in months. She could barely carry the weight of the load, but the thought of finally having a full stomach at the end of the day was enough to give her the strength to keep going.

"How long do you think it'll take for them to start following us?" she asked as they reached the tree line of a golf course.

"If they're smart, never," Sterling Granger replied, running his thumb along the shoulder strap of his new hunting rifle.

"*If* they're smart," Keith Bowman echoed, his whiskey-cured voice dripping with doubt.

They stopped at the edge of a frosty creek, a cold winter's breath rippling across the lazy stream.

"This is the spot," Sterling declared, taking a moment to admire the green expanse of the golf course, as overgrown as it had become. "Watch your step."

Riley took a measured breath, a long plume of mist escaping her lips as she focused on her trail of boot prints in the shallow snow. Slowly, they began backpedaling, tracing over their tracks as best as they could.

This was the third time that they had double-backed and

changed direction.

If anyone planned on following them back to their camp, they'd be walking in circles until nightfall. And if the canvas of gray clouds hanging over Kansas was anything to go by, their tracks would be hidden underneath the snow again before their pursuers could stumble across the right path.

"Alright, enough fucking around, let's head back," Keith decided as they reached the snow-dusted asphalt. Taking the lead, he glanced over his shoulder at Riley, "What was that shit about a tour bus back in the garage?"

"No idea," she shrugged, falling into the single file formation along the side of the road. "Even if they were willing to talk about it, I wouldn't have trusted a word that came outta their mouths. People say some stupid shit when their lives are on the line. But those girls... plain stupid, through and through."

"You sure about that?" Sterling asked from the rear, gently dusting their boot prints with a branch cut from an evergreen shrub. "Sounded like you three were having a good conversation back there."

"Compared to listening to you, absolutely," Riley fired back with a chuckle.

"Don't act like you don't enjoy my stories about life on the ranch," he replied, his swift strokes scratching the surface of the street.

"Alright," she conceded, her backpack rustling as she glanced back over her shoulder. "That one time you caught a drunk up in the hayloft was... passable."

"*Passable*," he snorted, shaking his head with a nostalgic smile. "If you could've heard the stutters slurring outta his mouth while he was trying to explain just what the fuck he was doing up there with a fistful of shit-stained straw, I'll tell you, *passable* would've been the last thing on your mind."

"Reminds me of one New Year's Eve I spent working the beat," Keith chimed in from up ahead as they cut north-east towards another neighborhood that they had already combed through.

"If that's not a one-sentence contradiction, I don't know what is," Riley remarked behind him. "You're the last person I'd expect to work on New Year's."

"This was before your skinny ass slipped outta the womb," Keith spoke over his shoulder, slowing his pace as his ropey frame attempted to reclaim his macho swagger, "Back when me and Nolan were still earning our stripes."

"I'm listening," Riley was intrigued now – her father had never talked much about his early years on the force.

"We pull up outside this restaurant," he began setting the scene. "Must've been two minutes until the fireworks. This one guy – booked the whole upper deck for his sales team. Restaurant manager says they've been up there since lunch. So you already know, this guy is fucked up beyond belief. Anyway, he comes outta the bathroom, and I shit you not, he's got a cantaloupe the size of a bowling ball bulging outta his ass, and he yells, *it's time for the countdown!!*"

"Get the fuck – no way," she laughed as they turned north, "What did Dad say?"

"Well, you gotta remember, this was before either of us had any sense," Keith stopped, turning back to grin at Riley and Sterling. "Nolan said, *ten, nine, eight…*"

The three of them burst out laughing, the sound of their voices breathing new life into the derelict neighborhood.

"Now, how'd you know that melon was the size of a bowling ball?" Sterling probed, tossing aside his branch.

"How you think?" Keith asked as the snow-dusted asphalt gave way to a dirt road, "Worst fucking start to the New Year I've ever seen."

"I'll tell you what, Keith," Sterling said as they neared an intersection, "You start telling a couple more of them cop stories by the fire, we'll get down to Texas in no time."

"First and last, amigo," he replied, pausing at the edge of the highway. "Your donkey-ass laugh's bound to get us all caught and killed."

They checked up and down the long stretch of road, but they weren't just looking for vehicles. They were looking for people – a travel-worn hiker, a family pushing a shopping cart, even a group of kids riding bicycles.

At this point, anyone who they encountered on the road was bound to be a threat or a burden, and with their backpacks full of supplies, they had no desire to meet either one.

"I was thinking," Riley began as they crossed the highway and cut through the eastern red cedars on the other side, "Maybe we should pull up our stakes and head somewhere outta walking distance."

"No, we're in a good spot right where we're at," Sterling spoke from behind as they navigated a path through the dense trees and scrub, taking care not to shake the snow from the branches. "We got a stripped vineyard to the east, burnt campground to the north, and a highway cutting down the west. Me and Jesse already checked these woods with the flashlights – we could build a big-ass bonfire and nobody would see a thing."

"What if we pulled back to our last camp?" Riley asked, despite the amount of fuel that they would have to burn. "I really don't wanna wake up to the people we just robbed trying to take their shit back."

"I'm siding with Sterling on this one," Keith called over his shoulder. "It'll be dark soon. If we leave now, anybody watching the roads are gonna see our headlights long before those kids see our tracks... But if they do find us, we shoot to kill."

CHAPTER 7

"Peanut butter and pickles!" Susan Armstrong crowed happily over the haul, holding her swollen belly with delight. "I've been craving this combination for as long as I can remember."

"Lucky you," Abbie Granger sighed enviously, the dark-haired rosy-cheeked woman smiling wistfully as they continued unpacking the three backpacks. "My order's a little harder to fill. Spicy fried fish drowning in lemon juice, with a chocolate-dusted caramel milkshake to wash it down."

The two pot-bellied pregnant women were sitting together on a picnic blanket, with their backs resting against the side of Virge's burly red minivan as they laid out the food.

Despite being the only two people with full stomachs in the group, Susan and Abbie had the first pick of the provisions while the others patrolled the perimeter.

The moment that their symptoms of morning sickness had started, the group had unanimously decided that the pair of expecting mothers were to be kept well-fed at all times.

And although the decision sometimes meant that everyone else would have to subsist on whatever else they could find, rationing a smaller and separate stockpile of supplies between themselves whenever food became scarce, it was a sacrifice that they had all agreed to make.

The growing babies shouldn't have to suffer just because of the world that they were being born into.

Having volunteered to dig the fire hole for the night, Riley tossed another scoop of dirt over her shoulder. Working in the long shadow of an evergreen eastern red cedar, the exertion of shoveling the cold hard ground was the perfect cover for the frown of resentment darkening her face.

After what the pair of women had done to earn their places among the cult community in Lake Springworth, Riley was finding herself increasingly unable to look at either of them without tasting bitterness – and she suspected that her aversion would only worsen as their pregnancies progressed.

She was sure that most of the others felt exactly the same way.

Sterling, however, was looking forward to becoming a father.

Looking past the circumstances of how it had happened, he considered the baby to be a blessing. He and his wife had admitted that they'd had difficulty with trying to conceive in the past – even IVF treatments hadn't worked for them.

Doctor Quinn had managed to help two people after all, at least before her feet had stopped twitching.

"Still don't get why you wanted a Dakota Fire Hole," Virge Norton's baritone voice ripped Riley from her remorseless reflection as he wheeled towards her.

The pronounced cheekbones in his ruddy complexion gave a bulging appearance to his keen eyes. Out of the group of seven, the grizzled war veteran had passed on most of their meager meals, insisting that sitting down in a chair all day meant that he could survive on half-rations for longer than any of them.

"I don't wanna take any chances tonight," Riley replied as she reared upright to stretch her back.

"That's deep enough," Virge's dog tags jingled over his army fatigues as he leaned over to examine the hole in the ground. "Start on the next one."

"I know Sterling and Jesse already checked the perimeter," she continued as she began working on the vent shaft. With her back to the wind, she dug diagonally towards the bottom of the first hole. "But it doesn't matter how thick the trees are around here, anyone can see smoke from a distance."

"Gonna be cold," he brooded in his chair as he glanced around at the fine layer of snow carpeting the ground. "I was looking forward to a decent bonfire for a change."

"Well, now you can look forward to waking up alive tomorrow," she gave him a small snort as she levered out another scoop of dirt.

"Only if we don't freeze to death tonight," he grumbled, his wary gaze sliding sideways towards the two pregnant women sitting beside his minivan. "How's it looking, ladies? We got enough food to get us down to Texas without making any more pit stops?"

"I think so," Susan reported with a glad smile, raising her eyebrows as she unzipped the third backpack. "This should hold us over for another month, at least."

"Good – means we can get outta this fucking weather," Virge scratched his beard with a discontented scowl. "I say we leave in the morning."

"No complaints from me," Abbie clambered to her feet with a few packets of beef jerky. "I'm gonna go give the boys a snack while they're waiting on dinner. Thanks again for bringing home the bacon, Riley."

"Don't mention it," she replied, focusing on her work so that she wouldn't have to make eye contact.

Planting her shovel's blade into the ground, Riley knelt down to peer at the bottom of the vent shaft.

She was almost through to the other side.

Taking care not to collapse the tunnel, she dug the rest out with her gloved hands.

"You two should eat something," Susan called from the picnic blanket.

"I'll wait until dinner's ready," Riley replied out of the side of her mouth, despite the hunger kicking inside her stomach. Looking up at Virge, she asked, "Where'd you put the kindling?"

"Somewhere you won't find it," he studied her with his scrutinizing squint. "Go eat. I'll build the fire."

A cloud of mist escaped her lips as she sighed begrudgingly, narrowing her eyes at the stubborn old man before climbing to her feet.

"Take your pick," Susan smiled warmly as her daughter drew closer, waving her hand over the abundance of food.

Riley's mouth salivated at the mere sight of the boxes of cereal flakes and muesli bars, jars of breakfast spreads and preserves, cans of tuna and corn, packets of dried fruit and nuts, bags of chips and chocolate, stacked in between piles of flour, pasta, oats and rice.

Her adrenaline had stolen her hunger back when she and Keith had been filling their backpacks. But seeing it all laid out before her now, she couldn't help but fall to her knees and descend on the closest thing to hand, struggling to open a box of muesli bars with her gloved fingers.

"Here," Susan offered with a sympathetic gaze, peeling a muesli bar open and holding it out, "Happy birthday, Riley."

"Birthday?" she echoed as she seized the bar, rending half of the honey-coated rolled oats and dried apricot in one bite. Chewing around her mouthful, she asked with furrowed eyebrows, "How do you know what date it is?"

"I don't," Susan admitted with a sheepish smile. "I just remember, every time your grandma would call to wish you a happy birthday, she would always say that it just started snowing outside, and that she'd love to see you for Christmas."

"So you don't know," Riley swallowed her half-chewed mouthful and turned her face to the side. "Just like you don't know whose baby it is you're carrying."

"Riley! I –" her words caught in her throat, and she looked around the camp for support.

Whatever help she had been expecting, it certainly wasn't coming from Virge.

They had all sensed the tension building between the two Armstrong women over the past few weeks, and now it was finally coming to a head.

Whether he had heard Riley or not, all of Virge's attention was focused on building the fire.

"You're right," Susan spoke softly, looking down at her lap. "There's no way to know whose baby it is, but just like I told you before – I'm sure that it's Nolan's."

"How the hell can you be sure it's Dad's!?" Riley exploded, throwing the muesli bar to the ground, hungry as she was. "He was gone for *three months* before Shepherd showed up. You can't tell me that you didn't know you were pregnant that whole time. It's bullshit! Raping Keith was one thing – lying that it's Dad's makes it even worse."

"Is that why you've been avoiding me these past few weeks?" she studied the anger written across her daughter's face for a moment, swallowing in the strained silence. "Riley, I haven't had my period since we left Redhurst. I didn't pay much attention to it back then, because I've always had abnormal periods, especially when I'm stressed. And after we arrived at the farm, I was still dealing with the death of your father..."

"Don't try to make me feel sorry for you by bringing up Dad," Riley snapped, shaking her head in disdain. "That thing in there is either Dad's, or it isn't. And I'm pretty fucking sure I know which one it is."

"If I give birth in spring, then it's Nolan's baby," Susan pursed her lips as a tear tracked down her cheek. "And you'll be a big sister to the last gift your father left for us."

Riley's heart sank.

She wished that it was true.

But it didn't change the way that she felt every time she saw her mother's swollen belly.

"Listen," Susan brushed her cheek with a sniffle, "Let's just focus on getting down to Texas first, and then we'll see what happens, okay?"

"I wasn't sure how to tell you this," Riley snatched up the half-eaten muesli bar and rose to her feet. She drew a deep breath of brisk winter air, summoning her resolve before gazing down at her mother. "I'm not coming with you."

CHAPTER 8

"Don't be ridiculous," Susan Armstrong scolded her daughter, clambering to her feet with difficulty. "Where are you gonna go?"

"I just wanna go home," Riley murmured, holding what was left of the muesli bar in her gloved hand. "That prisoner back in Lake Springworth said that Redhurst survived the asteroid. There's a good chance our house is still standing."

"And there's an even better chance that it isn't," Susan folded her arms. "You heard what he said about the riots and the break-ins. Looters would've turned the place over in the first week. There's nothing left for us back there."

"Our old family photos are still up in the attic," she replied with confidence. It was a guess, but she doubted that any scavengers would waste precious bag space with albums of somebody else's family. "I want a picture of Dad."

"Riley, you need to think this through," Susan glanced up at the darkening sky as the night began to settle in. "I wish I had a picture of Nolan too, but old photos aren't worth risking your life over. How are you even gonna survive out there on your own?"

As if to punctuate her question, a pair of boot heels scuffed the ground nearby, both women jerking their heads towards the noise.

Keith Bowman appeared at the edge of the woods, rounding the dirt road and striding into the camp, checking on Virge as the grizzled man fanned the flames in the fire hole.

"I've survived pretty well so far," Riley returned to the conversation, glancing pointedly down at the bounty of food laid out across the picnic blanket. "And besides, I won't be alone. I'll have Keith and Jesse with me."

"This is all your idea, isn't it?" Susan whirled on Keith with an accusing glare. "How dare you try to take my daughter away from me!?"

"I told Riley I was leaving," he stood beside the crackling campfire, his stony gaze going to the ground at Susan's feet. "She said she wanted to come – as long as we made sure you had enough food and fuel to get by without us."

"Well, thanks for your consideration, but –"

"I didn't get all that shit for you," he cut her off, nodding towards Riley as he advanced towards them. "I did it because she asked me to. I did it because I owed her, Sterling and Virge for saving me from that fucking prison. For saving me from you."

Susan shrank away from him as his boots padded onto the picnic blanket, but he only had eyes for the food.

He squatted down to snatch up a couple cans of baked beans before retreating back to Virge.

"I don't want you going with him," Susan whispered to her daughter, a hint of alarm in her voice. "He's not the same man we used to know."

Riley crushed the muesli bar in her hand as a sudden

sickening image flashed across her mind's eye – her mother spreading her thighs to mount Keith while he shouted and struggled in protest, chained up to a hospital bed, hardened by a force-fed cocktail of drugs.

"That's because you raped him," Riley furrowed her eyebrows at the hurt on her mother's face, as if she had been the victim. "You and your bitch of a sister raped him. Imagine if it was the other way around, and he forced himself on you. Or imagine it was me on that hospital bed, and someone I've known for as long as I can remember took advantage of me. Do you really think I'd ever be the same fucking person again!?"

"It's over now," Susan mumbled softly, her face drawn. "None of us can change what happened back there, no matter how much we wish we could." She took a deep breath before looking up at Riley again, "But we can change what happens next. When we get down to Texas, we'll have everything we need to settle down and start over – and maybe we can even start living normal lives again... just like we did at your grandma's."

Riley stood in silence as darkness descended over the camp.

The orange glow from the fire hole flickered briefly before Keith began frying the baked beans, thin wisps of smoke floating up into the evergreen foliage of the red cedar.

Illuminated by the flames, Virge's scrutinizing squint slid sideways towards the pair of women, having eavesdropped on their conversation – probably from the very beginning.

All of their ears strained to hear Riley's decision.

"Fuck living normal lives," she finally spoke, turning back to the shadow of her mother. "I can't look at you without remembering what you did to Keith. We're gonna divvy up the supplies tonight and head out in the morning."

CHAPTER 9

"May as well be driving three starry-eyed pups down to Texas," Virge Norton grumbled as he hoisted himself up into the driver's seat of his burly red minivan. "All this fucking *we're off to start a new life* bullshit. Makes me sick."

"Wasn't Texas your idea?" Riley Armstrong shot him a puzzled expression. "If you've changed your mind, you don't have to go."

"You know something," he began, glancing up at the morning rays of pale winter sun filtering through the frosty trees, "I'd rather freeze my nuts off and suck on stones for three square meals with the rest of you ass-monkeys. Sure beats spending the next six months listening to those two women coo and caw over whose little fucker's kicking harder."

"You make it sound like you're missing out on a good time," Riley chuckled, just now realizing how much she was going to miss the brooding old man. "Why don't you come with us instead?"

"Because nobody's driving this bitch but me," his arm slumped over the steering wheel with a resigned sigh. "And I'm not about to leave a pair of pregnant women in the rearview."

Riley knew how particular he was about his minivan.

Even with its shattered passenger window, as well as the rear window, he still refused to switch vehicles and let somebody else take over the driving. Insisting that there was nothing wrong with his minivan, he had sent her and Jesse to find some plastic sheets and tape them over the broken windows instead.

"Well, at least you'll have Sterling for company," she tried to give him something to lift his spirits, even though she knew that he'd still find a reason to complain.

Virge muttered under his breath, watching as the ex-rancher approached the burly red minivan with a pair of tent bags.

"Granger," Virge called him over, waiting until his face was in the plastic sheeting of the passenger window. "Let's get one thing straight before we leave – you try putting me on diaper duty for your spawn, and I swear, I'll drown you in the damn lake."

"This is gonna be a fun car ride," Sterling snorted, sharing an amused grin with Riley. "Hey, when you change your mind and you start walking down to Whistler's Valley, make sure you pick up a pistol for me on the way over. You still owe me for that one you lost back in Burview."

"It's not like you could ever hit anything with it anyway," she sassed him with half a smirk, before narrowing her eyes, having already given him the gun that she had taken from Heather. "I thought we settled that score yesterday."

"No, I earned that one," he corrected her, fingering at the hole in the chest of his green parka. "Damn near earned four."

"Whatever, I'll keep an eye out," she shook her head with a smile.

"Riley?" Abbie called from beside the fire hole, "When you're done over there, could you give me a hand with something?"

Sterling shrugged through the window, equally as clueless about what his wife wanted. He slid open the side door to continue loading up the minivan.

"Take care of my mom," Riley looked up at Virge, trusting that the grizzled war veteran would die to defend her if need be, despite his prickly facade.

"Yeah, yeah," he gave her a dismissive hand wave, his dog tags jingling as he leaned out to grab his wheelchair. "Do me a favor and don't die on the road. Crawl on over to the side first – makes for easier traveling for the rest of us."

"Good luck to you too," she gave him a small snort, closing his door halfway so that he wouldn't have to reach out so far for the handle. "Hey, maybe next time I see your van, you'll have the windows fixed."

"Ha," Virge grunted sourly, remembering the shootout that she had called down on his truck stop that had busted his minivan's windows in the first place. He stowed his collapsed chair into the compartment beside the center console before eyeing her again, "That reminds me, there's one more thing I wanted to say. When you get back to Redhurst, and you find your old photo albums up in the attic, and you're all depressed while you're flipping through the pages – make sure you don't forget to go fuck yourself."

Bursting into a chuckle, Riley crossed the clearing over to Abbie, who had just finished burying the remains of the fire hole.

"You should've waited," she furrowed her eyebrows at the pregnant woman. "I could've done that for you."

"I lived on a ranch before all this, I'm no stranger to hard work," Abbie panted slightly as she leaned on the shovel. "Besides, this isn't what I called you over for." She slipped a hand inside her checkered jacket's front pocket. "Here, come a little closer."

Riley glanced over her shoulder at the others, momentarily second-guessing the woman's intentions. Reminding herself that she held the physical advantage, she flexed her gloved fingers and took a few faltering steps forward.

"We're not gonna need these for a while," Abbie withdrew a pack of sanitary pads, subtly handing them over to her. "If you start getting cramps on the road, Keith and Jesse are gonna be lost at sea trying to find these for you."

"Thanks," she murmured, caught off guard. She stowed the pack into the front pocket of her gray hoodie, her supply running low. In all the excitement of finding a stash of food in the house that they had scavenged from yesterday, she had forgotten to check the bathrooms. "Are you guys gonna be okay when... the time comes?"

"Your mom's gonna give birth to that baby just fine," Abbie reassured her, seeing straight through the veil of the question. "Sterling and I have helped deliver well over a thousand newborns between the two of us. Granted, they were all calves, but I'd say we're a regular pair of obstetricians by now." She added with a smile, "And it won't cost a fortune in hospital fees either."

"Probably the next best thing after we burned down Quinn's lab," Riley supposed, not realizing how harsh the joke must have sounded until the smile on Abbie's face faded.

"Well, it looks like Susan's coming over," she quickly picked up the shovel, glad for an excuse to leave. "I'll give you two some privacy."

The two women passed each other with a friendly nod, Abbie climbing into the burly red minivan, glancing back at

Sterling as he checked over the empty campsite to make sure that he hadn't missed anything.

"There's nothing I can say to talk you outta this, is there?" Susan asked, already knowing the answer.

"I've had my mind made up for a while," Riley replied, idly stamping her boots over the dirt-filled fire hole. "We've been waiting forever to hit a haul like yesterday's, so I've had plenty of time to think it over."

"Then give me a hug before we leave," Susan yielded to her daughter's determination, extending her arms.

Riley kept herself from flinching, falling into her embrace.

She was still bothered by the swell of her mother's belly, but she didn't want to agitate her any further.

She wanted to part ways with her on good terms.

"You'll meet us in Whistler's Valley, won't you?" Susan whispered into her ear.

"Eventually," Riley promised, holding herself together in her mother's arms. "Just not until after you've had the baby."

"I'll be waiting," she murmured before drawing a deep breath. "There was a wedding photo on my dresser. If it's still there when you get home, would you mind bringing it back for me?"

"You got it, Mom," Riley nodded as she caught sight of Keith and Jesse rounding the edge of the woods into the clearing, returning from the final patrol around the perimeter. She gently pulled free of her mother, "It's time to go."

"You take care of yourself," Susan sniffed, gazing at her daughter one last time before turning back towards the idling minivan, brushing her wet cheeks as she went.

Riley stood beside Keith and Jesse as Virge swung around onto the dirt road, tires crunching out of the clearing.

Waving them off, she watched the plume of exhaust smoke

burn through the winter air until they disappeared around a bend.

Turning towards the wall of snow-dusted trees to the west, they adjusted the backpacks slung over their shoulders, and started on the long journey ahead.

With their two pistols, plus the shotgun from yesterday, they had three guns and a handful of ammunition to see them safely across four states.

And they had already pissed off the locals.

CHAPTER 10

"Barely a couple drops from that one," Jesse Bowman reported as he emerged from between a pair of yellow school buses, carrying two rubber hoses, a rag and a jerry can.

He was beanpole-thin underneath the folds of his brown fleece jacket, but compared to the boozed-up bundle of sallow skin and bones that he had been only a few months ago, he looked young and healthy again.

The occasional cluster of cars abandoned along the side of the highway were bone dry, so they had scaled a fence into the bus yard of an elementary school, hoping to score some liquid gold.

"Let me try the next one," mist emanated from Riley Armstrong's mouth, mingling with the frigid air as she stood beside the yard's fuel dispensers.

"Be my guest," he shrugged, holding out his makeshift siphoning kit.

She hung a defunct gas pump back on its cradle and crossed the snow-powdered parking lot. Plucking the longer length of hose from his hands, they walked around the side of the next bus.

"Somebody's already jimmied open all the fuel doors," Jesse began as he kicked a discarded fuel cap along the snowy concrete, "But it doesn't hurt to check anyway."

"Maybe we'll get lucky," Riley agreed as she fed the rubber hose down the filler pipe. "Whoever hit this yard first wouldn't have been too concerned about leaving the dregs behind."

Feeling the hose scrape the bottom of the tank, she took the smaller tube from Jesse and wedged it in beside the first one. Wrapping both pieces of plastic with the rag and packing it tightly over the hatch, she wiped the rim of the smaller tube with her gloved hand and blew inside.

A scanty snake of diesel twisted down through the longer hose, trickling into the jerry can before dripping dry, stopping just as suddenly as it had begun.

"More than the last one, at least," Jesse tried to sound hopeful, gathering up the tools again and starting towards the next bus.

They took turns siphoning, with Riley gazing up and down the highway while Jesse worked.

Out of the original seven who had fled California, only three were returning.

Nolan Armstrong was gone.

Stuart and Karen Sinclair were dead.

Even Hayden Marsh's group of six were out of the picture.

And now Susan was on her way down to Whistler's Valley in Texas – a campground supposedly teeming with wildlife, where Virge had claimed that there was enough hunting and fishing to keep them fed all year round.

"No luck on finding a generator around here," Keith caught up with them beside the fuel tank of the last bus in the yard. Adjusting the strap of the shotgun slung over his shoulder, he added, "Even checked the clinic across the street. How'd you guys do?"

Jesse picked up the hollow jerry can and gave it a shake, the dregs barely making a *swish*.

"Fuck me," Keith sucked his front teeth and looked up at the gray clouds in the sky. "We'd make better time walking back to Redhurst at this rate."

"Probably should've divvied up the fuel as well," Riley said half-jokingly, but only half. "There's no way we're getting home without a car."

"Those two sisters we stole from yesterday," Keith turned to her, stroking the stubble across his jaw, "You think their group already cleaned this place out?"

"They had pretty much everything else," she shrugged, considering the possibility. "I didn't see any fuel cans though."

"I wasn't exactly looking after we found the food," he admitted truthfully, huffing a rueful cloud of breath. "Shit, we could've walked past a whole pile of jerry cans and I still wouldn't have noticed."

"Why don't we go back?" Jesse asked the question that was on both of their minds.

"Bad idea," Riley was the first to shut it down. "They'll have their guard up now. They were shooting to kill yesterday. We might not get so lucky next time."

"Yeah, I'm not risking it without Sterling," Keith agreed, shooting Riley half a grin. "That man's got a guardian angel on his shoulders. You see the look on Abbie's face last night when she saw that fucking bullet hole clean through his jacket?"

"She was pissed," Riley shared his chuckle, "No wonder you guys went out on patrol straight after we got back."

"Dad, I can handle it," Jesse interrupted, his head turning between the two. "It's just the three of us out here now. You're gonna have to trust me when it comes to going up against other groups. Otherwise we're gonna run outta food long before we can find enough fuel to get us halfway back to Redhurst."

"Okay, let's say we can get enough fuel to fill up a tanker," Keith leveled his stony gaze at his son. "All that gas is gonna be worthless if we can't get a car battery to run. If something happens to you, who else is gonna get us back on the road?"

"That's easy," he argued, surprised that they didn't know. "All you need to do is find a trickle charger, plug in the battery, and hook it up to a power source."

"Easy for you, Jesse," Riley sided with Keith. "I don't even know what the fuck a trickle charger is."

She was lying.

She knew what it was.

She just wanted to hammer home how important Jesse was to the group.

It was a long hike back to California, and their only ride had already left for Texas.

"We're wasting time here," Keith decided after a brief stretch of silence. "Let's keep heading southwest. We just need to get outta this neighborhood, and then we can start checking for fuel again."

Jesse sighed a long plume of mist before nodding in agreement. He unshouldered his backpack and stowed his rag and rubber tubes inside.

Riley gazed out at the highway again, wondering just how far they'd have to walk before they'd come across an untapped supply of fuel.

She was considering the likely places that other groups of scavengers hadn't already hit, when a vehicle's engine interrupted her thoughts.

51

Turning slowly on the spot, trying to pinpoint the noise, she caught a glimpse of a black and white bus in the distance, cruising up the avenue.

It looked like it was a tour bus, and it was heading their way.

CHAPTER 11

"Shit," Riley breathed, ducking behind the row of yellow school buses.

"Alright, stay low," Keith murmured as the noise from the approaching vehicle grew louder. "It's probably just passing through."

The *thrum* of the engine changed, and Jesse's ears pricked up.

"Exhaust brakes," he whispered, frowning at the snow-powdered ground as he listened. "They're slowing down."

Sure enough, they heard the tour bus rumble to a stop just outside the concrete yard. The sound of its door opening hissed and popped above the idling engine, and heavy foot-steps scuffed the asphalt.

"We got one set of tracks heading towards the clinic!" a deep-voiced woman yelled. "Back it up, let's see what we can find!"

"Fuck, that was me," Keith clenched his jaw, his stony gaze going to the footprints that they had left all around the bus yard's snow-coated surface. "We gotta move."

Getting down on her hands and knees, Riley put her ear to

the ground, looking underneath the row of school buses.

High-pitched bleeps pierced the pulse pounding in her ears as the tour bus reversed along the avenue.

Like a curtain being drawn back, the vehicle unveiled sets of white and gray camouflage pants and tan-colored combat boots moving towards the parking lot across the street.

"Where do we go?" Jesse asked, glancing sidelong at his father.

Behind them was the elementary school's oval.

To their left was the empty staff parking lot.

And to their right was the highway running north to south.

The only structure in sight was the pedestrian walkway crossing over the highway, but that was on the corner of the avenue, and there was a long stretch of empty space in between.

"We're gonna have to run no matter which way we go," Riley exhaled as she stood upright, keeping her head below the school bus's row of windows. "I say we go for the walkway and hope they don't see us. If we can make it to the tree line on the other side of the highway, we can lose the tour bus."

"Good plan," Keith nodded, edging along the side of the school bus towards the rear. He whispered over his shoulder to Jesse, "Stay low and stay quiet. Let's go."

The chain-linked fence rattled as they scaled the mesh, with Jesse passing the jerry can up to Riley before climbing over.

Tightening the strap of the shotgun slung over his shoulder, Keith whipped out his pistol, waiting for the other two to land before they dashed across the highway's grassy shoulder.

Riley was the first to reach the base of the spiraling pedestrian walkway.

Crouching behind the cover of the concrete corkscrew ramp,

she peered between the railings at the group investigating their tracks.

They appeared to be soldiers, each of them wearing a winter camouflage uniform and carrying an assault rifle.

And they were already heading back towards the bus yard.

Thankfully, they hadn't noticed the flash of movement across the highway's grassy shoulder – but it wouldn't take long for them to pick up the tracks.

Still using the base of the pedestrian walkway for cover, Riley, Keith and Jesse sprinted across the road, leaping over a waist-high chain-linked fence and crashing into a crowd of winter-bare trees on the other side.

Bony branches and overgrown brush clawed at their clothes, puffs of snow shaking and spraying from the boughs as they passed.

Riley held the jerry can up to shield her face, following the heels of Jesse's shoes as they tore up clumps and sods of dewy vegetation.

Trailblazing their path through the trees, Keith suddenly switched directions, turning on a dime so that they wouldn't have their backs exposed to the highway.

Still running straight ahead, Riley lost sight of Jesse's shoes.

She lowered the jerry can just in time to see a thick branch waiting to clothesline her.

Pupils dilating, she skidded to a stop, a quarter-inch from a concussion.

Panting lungfuls of frigid air that misted in front of her face, she stared around at the tangle of trees, searching for signs of Keith and Jesse.

Away in the distance, the soldiers were already splitting off into two groups – one heading back towards the tour bus, while the other climbed over the concrete yard's fence, following the tracks in the snow.

"Fuck," Riley muttered to herself, unable to call out to the others without giving away her position.

She only had one choice – keep moving forward.

Ducking underneath the thick branch, she stumbled through the forest, hacking at the overgrown brush with one gloved hand until she caught a break in the trees up ahead.

Running parallel to the highway behind her, a set of train tracks lay littered with dead leaves and overgrown weeds growing among the gravel.

Scrambling up the rise, she turned south and sprinted down the tracks, determined to stretch the distance in between her and the soldiers, before the railroad's clear line of sight would force her to break off into the trees on the other side again.

Her boots drummed along the weathered wooden planks, matching the rhythm of her heart hammering in her chest. The dregs of diesel inside the jerry can swished and sloshed as it swung to and fro.

With a wide-eyed glance over her shoulder, Riley was about to jump off the tracks, when she glimpsed the outline of a man charging through the trees towards her.

An icy shot of adrenaline surged through her veins.

Tossing the jerry can aside to whip out her pistol, Riley dropped to one knee and flipped the safety lever off.

Puffing shallow breaths, she rested her left elbow on top of her thigh, pulling the gun up until she was staring along the top of the barrel.

"Shit!" Keith Bowman shouted as he burst through the trees, his own handgun jerking up halfway at the sight of her pistol pointed squarely at his chest. He spun around as Jesse emerged behind him before looking back up at Riley, "How the fuck did you get in front of us?"

"Took a shortcut," she flicked the safety lever back on, standing upright to slide the pistol into the waistband of her jeans at the small of her back. "Half of them left the bus. They're coming after us on foot."

"Who the hell are these guys?" Jesse asked as he snatched up the jerry can, following on the heels of his father as they crashed into the trees on the other side of the train tracks.

"That group we stole from yesterday," Riley began to explain, shielding her face from the branches with her gloved hands held up on either side this time, "They said something about a tour bus. If they were afraid of the soldiers, there's probably a good reason for us to be afraid too."

"*Soldiers?*" Jesse echoed in disbelief, "Why would they be chasing us?"

"I don't know," her guess was as good as his. She didn't even know whether they were really soldiers, or just another paramilitary pack of pricks playing the part. "You're welcome to stop and find out though."

"Save your breath," Keith called back as they broke into a clearing of overgrown grass, "You're gonna need it for the ball-squashing swamp crotch marathon we're about to run. The longer we outlast them on foot, the quicker they'll get back on their bus and fuck off."

Choosing speed over stealth, they trampled through the tall stalks of grass, cutting across the field and turning south down a narrow lane.

Coming across a handful of isolated homes, they swung left onto a driveway, jogging around a garage into a backyard and treading over untended flowerbeds and garden plots. Behind the property, back roads and bike paths snaked haphazardly between thickets of trees.

The contents of their backpacks rustled and bounced as they continued east, skirting around the edge of a lake towards an affluent neighborhood in the distance.

Abounding in horseshoe driveways hidden behind ornate gates and hedges, triple garages attached to multi-story houses, and a private lake for almost every home, Riley supposed that the wealthy locale had been a habitat for the rich and powerful.

Huffing and puffing through the spacious streets, she wondered whether the country's upper class citizens had gone to ground when the news of the approaching asteroid had reached them, hiding in their million-dollar bug-out shelters until somebody else cleaned up the mess and it was safe to emerge again.

Or maybe they had stayed behind, dying to defend what they had won off the hard work of others, rather than part with a single possession.

In either case, it was too bad that all of the windows had already been broken – she wouldn't be able to break one for herself.

"You hear that?" Keith held up his hand, stopping in the middle of the street.

Riley doubled over at the waist, hands on her knees as she caught her breath.

Her ears were stinging from running in the winter wind, but concentrating, she could still hear the *thrum* of the tour bus's engine closing in on them.

CHAPTER 12

"How the hell are they still on our tail?" Riley Armstrong panted, glancing back at Jesse.

She didn't expect him to know the answer, but vehicles were his area of expertise.

"Whoever they've got on foot must be giving them directions," he guessed, frowning at the ground as he tried to determine how far away the tour bus was.

"We can't outrun a vehicle," Keith Bowman conceded, turning his stony gaze towards a nearby driveway. "We might be able to throw them off our trail though."

The narrow driveway threaded in between two walls of bare-branched trees, the forest on either side forming a natural yet ominous archway. Gnarled winter fingers steepled above the lane, traveling around a corner and out of sight.

"We don't have time for a bait and switch," Riley reminded him as they ventured down the driveway that seemed to squeeze in on them from both sides. "They could be right around the corner back there."

"This is a choke-point," he replied, ducking underneath an overgrown branch as they jogged around a bend. "If I was chasing somebody down, I'd take my time coming through here."

Riley trusted in the former police officer's instincts, following his footsteps as he took a wide berth around the front entrance of a majestic three-story house.

The trio stood side by side, gazing up at the stately residence.

The century-old architecture had been spared the worst of the vandalism that had swept across the rest of the wealthy neighborhood – although it hadn't been particularly untouched by the chaos. The windows were boarded up and barricaded, scrawls of graffiti warned trespassers to turn back, and bullet holes riddled the brick walls of the upper levels.

It was possible that the owners had put up a vicious fight here before being gunned down, with the victors moving in and taking up residence until their supplies ran dry.

Riley could only assume that the place was abandoned now – simply because they weren't being shot to shreds where they stood.

"This is the spot," Keith nodded in agreement with himself, taking long strides towards the arched entrance's double doors. Reaching the threshold, he began backpedaling, "Watch your step."

Slow to catch on, Jesse clumsily traced back over his own footprints in the sprinkling of snow, joining Riley and Keith exactly where they had been standing only a few moments ago. He shot them both a frown of confusion before glancing nervously down the driveway again.

Riley was the first to slip backwards through the brush and trees lining the property, taking care not to leave any obvious entry tracks for the soldiers to find.

As far as their pursuers would be able to tell, their fleeing victims had just holed up in a post-apocalyptic fortress, and whatever the soldiers' intentions were, they would be forced to stop and reconsider their angle of approach.

Riley, Keith and Jesse tiptoed through the tree line, careful to avoid disturbing the dusting of snow that had settled on the shrubs that were too stubborn to die for the winter.

Slowly, the web of bare branches opened up to reveal an enormous pasture on the other side of the thicket, the rectangular meadow bordered on all sides by the galvanized steel mesh of a field fence.

"I can see houses on the other side," Jesse said in a low voice as he squinted at the line of trees in the distance. "Should we run across and find a place to hide? Looks like it'll be dark soon."

"Yeah, but we need to stay outta the open," Keith stroked his stubbled jaw as his stony eyes traced a route around the pasture. He shook his head, "Closest way across means we'd have to double-back the way we came."

"Didn't Sterling say his ranch looked something like this?" Riley furrowed her eyebrows as she spread her gloved hands along the top of the field fence's wooden rail.

"You mean a big-ass stretch of grass?" Keith shot her a skeptical sidelong glance. "This isn't exactly Nowheresville, Nebraska. After the neighborhood we just ran through, I'd bet any money – this land was about to get turned into a housing development."

"I'll take you up on that bet," Riley replied as she turned south, following the fence line. "You can keep your money though. Loser's cooking dinner in the barn tonight."

"That's a raw deal for me," Keith complained as he and Jesse trailed behind. "If I lose, I end up cooking two nights in a row.

And if you end up cooking, we all lose."

"Guess you better hope you're wrong then," she glanced back over her shoulder with half a smirk.

"What if you're both wrong?" Jesse piped up from the back.

"That's the best case scenario," Keith replied, grinning to himself, "Because that means your questioning-ass is cooking."

The trees began to thin out along the border of the field fence as they walked, giving way to the sight of a smaller adjoining property.

Riley paused beside the last tree to savor the look of defeat on Keith's face.

A wooden horse corral and stables stood on either side of the livestock gate that was connected to the grazing pasture, the glossy varnish of the buildings giving off a burnt sheen even in the winter's setting sun. The caretaker's quarters sat opposite a cavernous wooden barn, along with a sand-surfaced dressage arena in the back corner of the property.

"Fucking rich people," Keith muttered under his breath as they left the cover of the trees, scaling the fence into the back of the adjoining property.

Keeping a wary eye on the highway in the distance, they crept towards the rear of the caretaker's lodge.

No whinnies went up from the stables – the stalls had all been left open, their doors occasionally banging in the brisk breeze, the custodian having released the animals before abandoning the farm.

"Do you smell that?" Jesse paused, frowning. He turned towards the barn, "Do you think horse farms need tractors?"

Riley cocked her head in confusion, trying to draw the connection between his questions, when she picked up on the sulfurous scent of diesel wafting through the air.

Pivoting, they advanced on the cavernous barn instead, with Jesse leading the way, holding his jerry can.

Approaching the rear door, Keith purposely cut across his son's path.

The veteran policeman pressed his shoulder into the wooden wall of the barn – his pistol drawn and ready – before giving Jesse a terse nod to throw open the entrance.

By the time Riley had whipped out her own handgun, Keith had already slipped inside, sweeping the barn with his weapon, checking corners and scanning high and low for any signs of squatters.

"Clear," he reported, lifting one side of his fur-lined leather aviator jacket to holster his handgun again. "You're not gonna believe this shit."

The cavernous inside of the rustic barn was blissfully warm, owing to the stacks of hay bales lining the walls. Beside the front entrance, wheelbarrows were brimming with tools, while a battle-scarred workbench stood filmed with dust.

But in the center of the barn's hay-strewn floor was a cluster of red barrels – each of them exuding the tantalizing yet toxic fumes of diesel.

"Who the hell would leave all this here?" Riley put their thoughts into words, sliding her pistol into the waistband of her jeans at the small of her back.

They didn't have to wonder for long.

Like a faint howl on the wind, the dreaded *thrum* of the tour bus's engine returned.

CHAPTER 13

"So much for throwing them off our trail," Riley Armstrong seethed as they peered between the planks of the cavernous barn's wooden walls. "We may as well hold up a banner that says *Welcome Home.*"

A screen door slammed as the black and white tour bus rumbled up the long driveway, and a pair of winter-camouflaged soldiers emerged from the caretaker's lodge.

One man went to greet the bus, while the other began patrolling the perimeter, as if he had been outside all along.

"Maybe we can lie low up in the hay loft until they're gone," Jesse Bowman whispered from beside the cluster of diesel drums, jerking his head towards a ladder that led up to the barn's second level.

"They'll see our tracks out back," Keith clenched his teeth as he watched the uniformed men and women climbing down from the tour bus. The muscles of his square jaw flexed as he spoke quietly over his shoulder, "I need you two at the rear door. Get ready to move."

"Give me a minute," Jesse murmured as he cranked a rotary pump that had been fitted to one of the barrels, filling up his jerry can.

"What are you gonna do?" Riley whispered, furrowing her eyebrows at Keith. "If you're planning on taking them on alone just to buy us some time, you're only gonna get yourself killed."

"What are *you* gonna do?" he echoed, grabbing her wrist before she could reach for the handle of her pistol. "There's a whole group of those fuckers out there carrying assault rifles, and we're standing in a barn full of diesel. You open up on them now, and we're all dead."

She held his stony gaze as she jerked her arm out of his grip, but she made no move to draw her weapon.

Sighing sourly, Riley turned back to the crack in between the wooden wall's planks.

Her heart froze in her chest as the patrolling soldier filled her vision.

The burly blonde-bearded grunt was only there for a split second before he passed by the barn, but for her, it felt like an eternity.

"Trask, report!" a hulking woman demanded as she stood beside the tour bus, her stern gaze on the other sentry striding down the driveway.

"All clear over here, Sarge," Trask's tan-colored combat boots scraped to a halt in front of the oxlike officer. "No rats to catch out in the cold."

"Don't be so sure," the butch sergeant replied, eyeing him closely before leading the way back up towards the caretaker's lodge. "Newman's team traced three rats nesting at the fallback position. We're gonna sit here until nightfall before we link up to flush them out."

"Shit," Riley breathed, glancing sidelong at Keith. "They're waiting back at that big house. Where are we gonna go?"

"Anywhere but here," he muttered, turning back towards the cluster of diesel barrels. "Jesse, you done?"

"Shame to leave the rest of this here," Jesse whispered as he screwed the cap back onto his jerry can. "Yeah, I'm ready. Let's go."

Ears pricking at every slight noise, they crept back towards the barn's rear door.

Riley cracked the latch open, her hands clammy beneath her gloves.

A frosty breath of frigid air blew in her face as she peered out at the back of the property.

There were no signs of any soldiers, but one moment of safety seldom promised another. Despite the darkening sky, their tracks snaking towards the barn were as clear as day.

Steadily edging sideways along the wall with Jesse in tow and Keith bringing up the rear, Riley set her sights on a row of trees lining the low fence of the horse farm's dressage arena.

Stifling her breath misting on the breeze, she checked around the corner of the barn.

Nothing.

Adrenaline spiking through her veins, she wrapped one arm around her backpack to hold its contents in place, before taking off at a sprint towards the nearest tree.

Jesse – still a rookie when it came to scavenger runs – was less than stealthy. His pack rustled and rattled with every footfall, diesel sloshing and gurgling around in his jerry can.

"HEY!!" a shout pierced through the icy chill of the approaching winter night.

Ducking low behind a tree trunk, Riley chanced a glance back at the barn, and her heart dropped to the pit of her stomach.

The patrolling sentry had turned the corner, catching Keith mid-dash.

Swinging up the barrel of an assault rifle, the blonde-bearded soldier held him at gunpoint.

CHAPTER 14

.

"One move and you'll bleed my name into the fucking snow, asshole!" the winter-camouflaged soldier warned, advancing with his assault rifle trained on Keith Bowman's fur-lined leather aviator jacket. "Toss your weapons, real slow."

"Make up your mind, you piss-bearded piece of shit," Keith growled back, frozen in place as his stony gaze followed the burly blonde man's approach. "You want me to stay still or not?"

"Riley, we've gotta do something," Jesse whispered in her ear as they watched from behind a tree trunk.

Before she could even consider an angle of attack, three more soldiers came around the corner of the barn, investigating the noise with their weapons raised.

"How many hostiles, Wheeler?" the butch woman called as they drew closer.

"Just the one, Sarge," he reported, staring along the top of his assault rifle's barrel.

"Listen, I'm not here for a fight," Keith declared, louder than he needed to. He held up his arms, surrendering himself willingly, "I'm outnumbered and outgunned. I'm gonna get

68

myself shot to shit before I even touch a trigger."

Furrowing her eyebrows, Riley realized that he wasn't just giving himself up.

He was telling her and Jesse to stand down.

Staying low behind the fence of the horse farm's dressage arena, with her stomach flat on the ground, Riley began crawling through the snowy overgrown grass, looking back over her shoulder to keep her eyes on the soldiers.

"Riley, where the fuck are you going?" Jesse mouthed silently at her before turning back to see his father getting stripped of his weapons.

He hadn't heard Keith's message.

She would have exhaled in exasperation, but she couldn't risk the mist of her breath betraying their position.

Waiting for Jesse to make eye contact with her again, she signaled for him to follow.

"Smart choice," the oxlike sergeant remarked as her soldiers secured Keith's pistol and shotgun. She placed her masculine hands on her robust hips, "But if you didn't come here to die, then what's got you sniffing around our supply depot?"

"This dick-freezing shit-steaming weather," Keith's hands were still raised as another soldier patted him down, searching for any other concealed weapons. "I was looking for somewhere warm for the night. I didn't know anyone else was –"

"You rats are all the same," the butch woman snorted, cutting across him as she squatted beside the other pair of tracks on the ground. She glanced up at the trees lining the dressage arena. "Take whatever you can get your filthy paws on, and then run at the first sign of trouble."

Sucking his front teeth, Keith stared up at the winter twilight painting purple across the sky, before hooking his thumbs into his belt loops.

"Who the fuck's running, bitch?" the vulgar veteran police officer challenged, his whiskey-cured voice rumbling into the night as he bought time for Riley and his son to escape. He chuckled to himself, "Oh, that's right – anybody unlucky enough to see your pushed-in hoof-chinned bushpig face."

"Fuck, Keith," Riley breathed, rising up on her hands and knees as they crawled behind a thicket of trees at the edge of the property.

The gleam of the sergeant's grin shone in the darkness as she balled a huge fist, hefting all of her hulking weight into a punch aimed at Keith's gut.

Three months ago, the former policeman could have taken the hit.

His broad-shouldered physique and beefy arms would have been more than enough to go pound for pound with the butch woman in a fair fight.

But the ropey remnants of the half-starved man's muscles were no match for the sergeant, and one gut-punch from the oxlike officer was enough to make him double over, spit stringing from his mouth.

One soldier kicked out the back of his knees, bringing him to the ground, and another grunt clocked him across the jaw. Tan-colored combat boots rose and fell in the moonlight as they all took a shot at what was left of his defiance.

"Motherfuckers," Riley's gloved hand went to the waistband of her jeans at the small of her back, gripping the handle of her pistol.

"What are you waiting for?" Jesse seethed, clenching his fists. "Start fucking shooting."

"Is that – the best – you got!?" Keith roared between the soldiers' stomps, covering his head and neck with his arms, "I've seen – kids kick rocks – harder than you street-walking cheap-whoring queef-snorting cream-hawking cucks!"

Kids, kick rocks, Riley picked up on the inflection in his tone, releasing her grip on the hilt of her pistol.

"Jesse, we have to go," she urged, crouching beside the last tree as they reached the property's fence line.

"What about my dad?" he winced at the sound of his father's bellows, Keith determined to draw out the beating for as long as possible in between his coarse taunts.

"There's nothing we can do," Riley whispered back, grabbing Jesse's shoulder and turning him around to face her. "Not with one gun against a bunch of soldiers. If we try to save him now, we'll only end up getting ourselves caught, or we'll get him killed in the crossfire."

"They're already killing him," Jesse fumed, shaking out of her grip. "I'm not gonna sit here and watch them kick my dad to death."

"Come on, you pansy fuckers!" Keith barked, spitting blood at the whites and grays of their winter camouflage uniforms. "Don't tell me you're already getting tired. You fist-shitters are dropping off faster than your wives' panties at the neighborhood cookout!!"

"He's a tough son of a bitch," the butch woman admitted, extracting herself from the circle of stomping soldiers. "Throw him in the rat cage. Wheeler, go find the rest of his pack. Take Trask with you. We'll hold down the fort."

Riley and Jesse shrank towards the fence line as two of the grunts broke off the attack, following their tracks through the snow-powdered grass.

CHAPTER 15

"We're not leaving him back there," Jesse Bowman huffed as they climbed through yet another abandoned house's broken window.

"We'll get him back," Riley Armstrong promised, her heart thumping in her chest as they ventured down a dark hallway, "Just not tonight."

"Good," he followed her into the house's shadowy dining room, using the moonlight to navigate around the overturned table and chairs. "Because I remember what you said back when we left Lake Springworth – *we take who we need, leave who we don't*. You need me to start a car, but you don't need my dad."

"Don't be a fucking idiot," Riley whirled around, grabbing the collar of his brown fleece jacket and pulling him close. "We're gonna hit that farm tomorrow and get him back, but we need to be smart about it. I'm not going in guns blazing just because you're too impatient to let me put together a plan... And if it makes you feel any better – I need your dad more than I need you, because there's no way I'm making it back to Redhurst in one piece with *you* watching my back."

"Fine, we'll do it your way," Jesse knocked her gloved hand aside and sidled over to the dining room's broken back window, its weathered curtains flapping in the frosty breeze. He pulled them to one side and glanced back at her, "Hurry up."

Narrowing her eyes at him, Riley stepped out onto the back deck and climbed down into the overgrown yard.

A flurry of snow blew past her face as she gathered up her light brown ponytail and pulled her hood up over her ears, tugging the drawstrings tight against the frigid winter wind.

The contents of their backpacks rustled and rattled as they clambered over the back fence and into the woods behind the property.

Tramping through the bare trees until they eventually reached the fence of another forgotten former home, they double-backed and turned north, with Riley stooping to sweep their footprints with a fallen branch.

This was the fifth time that they had left false prints and changed direction.

She knew that the steady snowfall would soon cover up their tracks anyway, but she wanted to make it as difficult as possible for the stalking soldiers to trace their trail.

"What have you got for a plan so far?" Jesse asked as she took the lead again after a safe distance.

"Well, the first thing we need is more guns," she replied, tossing the branch into the moonlit trees. "Those two sisters we ran into yesterday knew about the tour bus. Maybe their group can help us."

"*Help us?*" he echoed incredulously, "We just stole half their shit. What makes you think they're not gonna *shoot* us?"

"Maybe the soldiers kidnapped some of their people too,"

Riley hoped. She knew from firsthand experience just how powerful the desire to rescue a lost loved one could be. "But if that's not enough to make up for yesterday, then we could offer to split the diesel and whatever other supplies those soldiers have got on that farm."

"That's if those sisters don't kill us on sight," Jesse sighed dejectedly, tramping through the snow-covered shrubs. "We should've waited until we were farther down south before we split off from the rest of the group. We could've avoided those soldiers completely, then we wouldn't have to deal with other scavengers we've already stolen from, and we'd be outta this freezing weather too."

"Should've, could've, would've," she shook her head in scorn, keeping her gaze focused on the stretching expanse of a moonlit golf course materializing beyond the trees. "If you've got a time machine, let me know. I'd go back to that first day, when Sinclair shot my dad on the roof of that parking garage."

"I'm sorry, I didn't mean –"

"It doesn't matter," she cut across his attempt to apologize, looking back at him as they reached the edge of the woods. "We can't change the shit that we're sinking in. The only thing we can do now is learn how to swim in it."

CHAPTER 16

The moon flew high in the winter sky, wreathing the golf course's grounds of overgrown grass in its pale glow. If Riley's sense of direction was correct, then this was the same golf course that she had come across yesterday with Keith and Sterling.

That meant that somewhere in one of the surrounding neighborhoods, Heather and Taylor were hunkered down in their barricaded double-story house – hopefully with more guns and enough friends in their group to make a difference in the fight against the soldiers.

Skirting around a sand bunker, Riley pushed the thought to the back of her mind as she and Jesse approached the country club on the top of the hill.

Cradling her pistol in both hands, she kept the barrel pointed at the ground as they prowled around the side of the building towards the front entrance.

Passing underneath the moonlit shadow of the prominent portico, they found both of the glass doors smashed, a gaping hole inviting them into the dark hallway beyond.

Like the specter of a clubhouse manager coming out to greet

them, an eerie breeze sighed through the wind tunnel of the foyer's corridor, brushing their faces with a frosty breath that was somehow even colder than the air outside.

"I wonder if we'll ever see a normal window again," Jesse remarked as they ventured inside, windswept glass crystals crunching underneath their shoes.

"If we do, I'm breaking it," Riley murmured, sweeping her handgun over the counter of the information desk.

They plunged deeper into the darkness of the clubhouse, treading on fallen picture frames and the scattered remnants of an overturned trophy case.

The contents of Jesse's jerry can sloshed and gurgled as he set it down on the carpet floor. Shrugging off his backpack, he unzipped the bag and rummaged around inside.

"What are you doing?" Riley bristled, glancing down at his silhouette in the middle of the bleak wind tunnel.

"Getting a flashlight," he whispered, clicking on a torch and shining the beam in her face.

"Are you a fucking idiot!?" she hissed, snatching the torch out of his grasp and switching it off again. Blinded by the sudden blaze of light, she stumbled backwards into a wall, reprimanding the spot that he had been crouching in, "You may as well paint a fucking bullseye on our backs. If those soldiers following us didn't just see that, then anyone who might be hiding in here would have. If I could see you right now, I'd beat your face in with this fucking thing."

"I'm sorry, I didn't realize," Jesse's hushed voice came from a completely different direction compared to where she was glaring.

"Just stop trying to get us both killed," Riley sighed in exasperation.

Waiting for her night sight to return, she listened to his movements as he quietly gathered up his supplies, his footfalls soon continuing down the corridor.

At this point, she couldn't have cared less if he was walking straight into an ambush.

For a guy who had only earlier pleaded with his father to trust him when it came to going up against other groups, he was certainly proving his uselessness in that regard.

Dark objects shimmering into focus again. Riley resumed her steady advance towards the shadowy lounge at the end of the hall.

To her left were two sets of change rooms and a flight of stairs.

To her right was the open doorway to the tiled corridor of a kitchen.

And straight ahead were the gloomy remains of the clubhouse's restaurant.

Shoving Jesse's flashlight into the front pocket of her gray hoodie, she swept her handgun over the restaurant's bar counter, before navigating her way past the splintered remnants of overturned tables and chairs.

Stepping over scattered golf balls and shattered glass, she ventured into the pale moonlight shining in through the broken windows.

A cold gust of musty wind blew against her hooded face as she stepped out onto a concrete terrace.

Beyond an array of wrecked sun lounges and outdoor tables that hosted snapped and hanging umbrella centerpieces, the clubhouse's stagnant swimming pool rippled in the winter breeze, giving off the earthy stench of green algae.

Checking the dingy pool house and the corners of the fenced

courtyard, Riley turned to head back inside, when she caught sight of a silhouette standing in the restaurant's row of broken windows, watching her.

She might have jerked her gun up if the shadow hadn't been carrying a jerry can.

"No sign of anybody in the kitchen or the change rooms," Jesse reported, bracing against the brisk breeze skimming off the stagnant pool water's scummy skin.

"Sure you don't wanna check the bar while we're here?" Riley prodded the former alcoholic, feeling the weight of his flashlight shifting in her hoodie's front pocket.

"Come on," he averted his gaze, turning back towards the restaurant. "We're past that."

"Just making sure," she replied, kicking golf balls aside as she took the lead back through the tangle of tables and chairs.

Cutting across the shadowy lounge in the hall, Riley ventured up the flight of stairs, both hands gripping her pistol's hilt, safety off, with her forefinger laid alongside the trigger guard.

Just like every other piece of glass that they had encountered in the state of Kansas, the panoramic window lining the entire upstairs function room had been shattered, the frigid winter wind tugging at the weathered linen of once-white tablecloths and chair covers.

A moldy three-tiered wedding cake sat uncut on a corner table, while broken wine bottles and scattered silverware littered the carpeted floor. The melted remains of a plastic trash can occupied the center of the function room, probably having served as the single-use indoor fire pit for another group of scavengers who had passed through.

Scanning the snow-sprinkled wooden balcony outside, Riley

swept her handgun behind the raided corner bar, coming across three doors at the end of a small passageway.

"You check the bathrooms," she whispered over her shoulder as she withdrew Jesse's flashlight.

Holding her pistol in one hand, she elbowed open the third door, peering into the darkness before clicking on the torch.

Her breath fogged across the flashlight's beam as she cast it over the function room's gloomy kitchenette, revealing a small counter and sink, a storage closet, and a dumb waiter embedded in the wall.

Finding the storage closet empty – save for a few bottles of cleaning chemicals lining the shelves – Riley waited for Jesse to come back from the bathrooms before finally allowing herself to relax.

"This is a good spot for tonight," she said as she unshouldered her backpack, propping it up on the counter. "You get started on dinner, I'll see if I can get a fire going."

Riley double-checked that the batteries had already been taken out of the clubhouse's smoke detectors, before gathering up small pieces of broken furniture to light a fire inside the dumb waiter's compartment.

"You think everybody survived?" Jesse asked as he stood by the bench, scooping out spoonfuls of canned tuna onto half a dozen crackers. "The people from the wedding reception, I mean."

"Probably," Riley shrugged, too preoccupied with pondering which way the fire's smoke would travel, and whether she would have to prop open the kitchenette's door to let it escape. "I didn't see any bodies out there, so that's probably a good sign."

"Did you see a lot of bodies whenever you were out scavenging with my dad?" he wondered, searching in vain for a bin to throw the empty tuna can.

"A couple," she nodded, remembering the pregnant woman wearing an orange summer dress, "There was this one yesterday –"

A wooden thud from somewhere outside cut their conversation short.

"Probably just the win–" Jesse tried to reason before Riley clamped her gloved hand over his mouth.

Another identical wooden thud resounded from just outside the function room.

CHAPTER 17

The rhythmic wooden thuds outside the function room's kitchenette grew in resonance with every ear-thundering heartbeat.

"You and your fucking flashlight," Riley Armstrong seethed as she hooked her arms through her backpack on the counter.

"What do we do?" Jesse Bowman panicked, his wild eyes darting from the fire in the dumb waiter's compartment to the kitchenette's service door.

"Make it look like we were never here," she hissed, grabbing three of the tuna crackers from the counter. Shoving her half of their dinner into her mouth, she shut the dumb waiter's hatch on the fledgling fire's flames.

Jesse stumbled around in the sudden darkness, waving his hands around the gloomy room to gather his bearings.

Riley forced her mouthful down before swiping the other three crackers off the bench, hiding Jesse's share of dinner as she hauled him across the room towards the storage closet.

"You think the soldiers found us?" Jesse asked as she dragged him inside.

With the second batch of tuna crackers in her mouth, she

was unable to form an answer – but even if she could, the only words that she had for Jesse were far from whatever response that he was expecting to hear.

Fishing the flashlight from the front pocket of her gray hoodie, Riley flicked on the torch and glanced around at their cramped surroundings. Shadows leapt from the shelves as she cast the beam of light over the few bottles of cleaning liquids.

Like a pair of rats, they were trapped inside the storage closet, with nowhere else to run.

Riley made eye contact with Jesse, his dilated pupils constricting in the torchlight as their breaths mingled in the small space. She found herself wondering when the last time was that either of them had brushed their teeth.

Her heart skipped a beat as a crunch of glass sounded from the function room outside, picturing the pair of soldiers who had tracked them all the way to the golf course's clubhouse.

She knew that her pistol would be no match for their assault rifles.

If the two grunts found them hiding in the kitchenette's storage closet, she would have a slight chance of killing one – but not the other.

They were backed into a corner now, and only certain death awaited them if they decided to put up a fight.

"The roof," Jesse whispered in sudden realization, seizing her wrist and pointing the flashlight's beam up at the ceiling panels. He clasped his hands together against his thigh, "Come on, I'll boost you up."

Holding the torch in between her teeth, Riley stepped up into his hands with her hiking boot.

His beanpole-thin arms struggled to support her weight, despite her half-starved figure.

Planting her other foot onto a shelf to shift some of the burden, she reached up to lift one of the ceiling panels, peering into the roof space's darkness for a viable handhold.

A door creaked open outside.

It was one of the bathrooms.

They were getting close.

"I'm losing my grip," Jesse's hushed voice strained behind clenched teeth, guiding her boot towards the same stack of shelves that she was standing on.

The rack began leaning sideways, two of its support legs lifting up off the floor.

Dropping the ceiling panel with a reverberating thud, Riley clawed at the top shelf to keep her balance, throwing her weight towards the wall in a desperate bid to prevent the rack from toppling over.

But it was too late.

With a metallic screech, the stack of shelves came crashing down, hurling Riley, bottles of cleaning chemicals and a cloud of dust onto Jesse, the flashlight's beam spinning out of reach as they both collapsed to the floor in a twisted heap.

The kitchenette's service door swung open, with another torch sweeping the room, its glow casting a menacing aura around the storage closet's door frame.

An icy spike of adrenaline surged through Riley's veins.

Writhing underneath the tangled mess, she managed to get an arm free, and she reached for her pistol in the waistband of her jeans at the small of her back.

But her gloved fingertips only scrabbled at empty denim.

The closet's door cracked open, and an overwhelming wave of panic washed over Riley as she flailed her arm around, bashing her hand into twisted shelves and scattered cleaning chemicals and Jesse's face in a desperate search for her gun.

Riley's breath froze in her chest as a flashlight shone in her eyes.

CHAPTER 18

"Is that Riley?" a familiar voice called, the flashlight's beam lingering on her face.

"I don't believe it," she pulled her hood back and shaded her eyes, staring up at the silhouette standing in the doorway. "Calvin!?"

"Surprised you still remember me," the torch's glare fell away with a flash of the young man's roguish grin, and he bent down to pull them up out of the wreckage.

"You know this guy?" Jesse asked in a daze, shaking dust from his tousled brown hair as Calvin helped him clamber to his feet.

"Yeah, we went to high school together," Riley answered as she shoved herself free of the twisted shelves, her racing heart slowing to a steady rhythm again. She picked up Jesse's fallen flashlight and found her pistol in the corner of the closet before facing them both. "Calvin Fisher, meet Jesse Bowman."

"Hell of a way to meet," Calvin chuckled, giving Jesse's hand a firm squeeze. "Don't tell me I gave you guys a scare?"

"No, we hang out in storage closets all the time," she sassed him, before considering the implications that the sentence carried. She would have rubbed the back of her neck if her hands weren't full. Stowing the pistol into the waistband of her jeans at the small of her back, she gave Calvin a hug before flipping the focus on him, "What the hell are you doing here?"

"I came to pick you up for brunch at the marina," he shot her half a smile with his cleft chin, waiting for her to remember.

It took a moment for Riley to realize, but just before her whole world had been turned upside down, she had planned to spend the day with Calvin. The last time that she had seen him was outside her house back in Redhurst, with Nolan Armstrong sending him off, one menacing hand gripping the hilt of his holstered service pistol.

She traced the torch's beam over his gunmetal gray ski jacket.

His easy blue eyes had hardened into a piercing gaze over the past six months, and he seemed more rugged than what she remembered, but underneath all that, he was still the same guy. Somehow through the apocalypse, he had managed to hold onto his boyish charm and his athletic build – he was even wearing his black fringe up after all this time.

"No, seriously, what the fuck are you doing here?" Jesse raised his eyebrows as he crossed the kitchenette, opening the dumb waiter's hatch and bathing the room in the orange glow of the fledgling flames within. He turned back to watch Calvin's face in the firelight, "Were you followed?"

"I don't think so – I mean, not that I was checking," he shrugged, his eyes going from Riley to Jesse and back again. "Feels like I've been on the road since this whole thing started. I was looking for somewhere warm to stay for the night, when I saw this flash of light coming from the clubhouse. I figured there might be some people here, so I came to check it out."

"I told you someone would see your torch," Riley shot an

accusing glare at Jesse before pocketing his flashlight again. She turned back to Calvin, "You hungry?"

"Yeah, I was just about to ask," he unshouldered his backpack and set it down on the floor, "What are you guys having for dinner?"

"Tuna crackers," Jesse jerked his head towards the kitchenette's empty counter, before realizing that the fruits of his labor had disappeared.

"Forget that," Calvin unzipped his bag and pulled out a pair of brown packets. "I scored a box full of MREs a while back. I've been saving these last two for a special occasion." He winked up at Riley as he began unwrapping the field rations, "It's not exactly brunch at the marina, but eating on the top floor of a golf course's clubhouse sure has a ring to it."

"Quit acting like you were saving them for me," Riley gave him a small snort. She watched the stack of food pouches tumbling out of the brown packaging onto the floor, and she started towards the service door, "I'll get us some pans from the kitchen downstairs."

"Nah, no need," Calvin replied, sorting through the pile and holding up a pair of green plastic bags. "They come with their own heaters. Just add a little water and they cook by themselves."

"Plates and cutlery, then," she persisted, examining the two ration packs before glancing over at Jesse, "So we can share."

"Don't worry about me," Jesse replied, standing beside the fire with his arms crossed. "I'm fine with tuna crackers."

"How come you're on your own?" Riley turned back to Calvin. "Are your parents okay?"

"They're gone," he swallowed, his gaze turning downcast, "Long story."

87

He avoided making eye contact for a while, instead focusing his attention on wedging the airtight meal pouches inside the pair of green bags. Pulling a canteen from his backpack, he added some water to each plastic bag and folded the tops down. He inserted both bags into two narrow cardboard cartons, and then propped them up on an angle against the wall.

"We've all got long stories," Jesse muttered, taking a withdrawn interest in how the meals were supposed to cook without coming anywhere near the fire.

"When you texted me about the asteroid," Calvin finally looked up at Riley, sitting beside the rations with his back against the wall, "I went straight home. It took me a while to convince my parents to take it seriously, so by the time we packed up and left, we got caught up in all the traffic, along with everybody else on the freeway."

"We saw how bad that was," Riley remembered standing at the edge of the parking garage's roof back in Redhurst, gazing at the miles of headlights and taillights lining the freeway in either direction. "You should've called me. We took the cemetery roads."

"I tried," he sighed, running a thumb along his jaw line, "Couldn't get through. Our phones just stopped working, and we couldn't get a signal – no matter how many times we tried rebooting."

"Same thing happened to us," Jesse remarked as he crossed the room to the counter, digging out a box of crackers and a fresh can of tuna from his backpack. "We had the sense to bring some walkies with us though, so we were fine."

"How did you get off the freeway?" Riley's question was for Calvin, but she furrowed her eyebrows at Jesse, wondering what his problem was.

"We didn't," Calvin answered, idly unwrapping the accessory packets from the MREs, "Not all of us, at least. We were having dinner on the side of the road, with a bunch of other people who were stuck in the traffic as well, when a gang of bikers showed up. They must've figured that while everyone else was caught up in the chaos, and with all the phones down, it was open season for crime."

"Back when people thought money was still important," Riley supposed, remembering the gunfire outside the pawn shop at a downtown strip mall.

"Anyone who fought back got shot," he continued, handing her a plastic spoon. "We thought we had the numbers on our side. It didn't matter. They killed my parents and left me for dead."

"I'm sorry," she offered her condolences as she sat down beside him. "What happened after that?"

"Luckily for me, one of the people we had dinner with was a nurse," he stared at the kitchenette's service door on the opposite wall, before gazing sidelong at Riley with his piercing blue eyes. "Ever since then, I've just been wandering around, hoping to find other survivors who haven't turned into complete animals."

"So you just walk up to strangers and hope they don't shoot you?" Jesse asked suspiciously, turning around with a tuna cracker raised halfway up to his mouth. "What happens if you run into the wrong people?"

"Guess my luck hasn't run out yet," he shrugged with a grim twist to his roguish grin. "To be honest, I feel like I was supposed to die with my parents on the side of that freeway. So I'm not letting the fear of death keep me away from some good company and a warm fire."

"Well, it looks like we both got lucky tonight," Riley turned between Jesse and Calvin, before nodding towards the storage closet. "Because if I hadn't dropped my gun in there, I would've shot you the second you opened up that door."

"Is that why you asked if I was being followed?" Calvin asked, holding her gaze for a moment before frowning up at Jesse. "Are you guys in some kinda trouble?"

"You could say that," Jesse snorted, swallowing his mouthful. He held up another tuna cracker, "Riley stole all this food from some of the local scavengers. And tomorrow, we're gonna go back and ask them for their help. But that's only if the soldiers don't find us first."

CHAPTER 19

Riley Armstrong lay awake underneath the dumb waiter's compartment, struggling to fall asleep, despite the calming orange glow emanating from the fire.

Maybe it was because of the cold hard tiles on the kitchenette's floor.

Maybe it was because of the scratchy weathered tablecloths from the function room.

Or maybe it had nothing to do with her makeshift bedding at all, and everything to do with Calvin Fisher quietly snoozing in the corner, only a few feet away.

From the moment that their meals had finished cooking, Riley had volunteered to take the first watch, choosing to eat outside to keep an eye on the golf course's grounds.

Naturally, Calvin had followed her out to keep her company, both of them swapping stories late into the night – some tragic, some comic – warming up to each other again with their bellies full of surprisingly good food.

After hearing about the situation between the scavengers and the soldiers, Calvin had been more than willing to help Riley and Jesse. He had even offered to personally smooth things over with Heather and Taylor's group, so that they could join forces to save Keith, along with whoever the two sisters might have lost.

But it was the guilt that was keeping Riley awake.

She couldn't help thinking that if she hadn't sent the text message to warn Calvin about the asteroid all those months ago, then he wouldn't have been stuck in traffic on the freeway, and then maybe his family would still be alive.

But on the other hand, if his parents hadn't been killed on that freeway, then he wouldn't have been wandering around aimlessly across the country, eventually crossing paths with Riley again, at a time when she needed all the help that she could get.

She didn't know what was worse – the guilt that helping him had resulted in the death of his parents, or the secret gladness that the death of his parents had resulted in him helping her.

And as if that wasn't already enough to grapple with, after everything that had happened, the asteroid hadn't even touched Redhurst.

The kitchenette's service door creaked, and her eyelids snapped open.

"I think I need to turn in for the night," Jesse Bowman yawned in the doorway, his weary face illuminated by the fire. "I feel like I'm about to fall asleep out there."

"Someone needs to keep watch," Riley reminded him. She sat up and hooked her arms through her backpack with a sigh, "May as well be me – I can't sleep anyway."

"I'll go," Calvin offered as he stirred in the winter wind pervading the room.

"You were already on first watch," she replied, furrowing her eyebrows as she realized that the same could have been said of her.

Maybe she was beginning to get tired after all.

"I've had a few good hours," Calvin flipped off his tablecloth blankets and stood with a stretch. "Besides, from the sound of things, we've got a big day tomorrow, and you guys need to be rested up as well."

Jesse stood to one side as Calvin grabbed his bag and left the room.

Riley settled back onto the floor again, using her backpack as a pillow.

Feeling the warmth from the fire return, her eyes lingered on the spot in the corner where Calvin had slept, until Jesse flopped down onto the pile of weathered linen making himself comfortable.

"I don't trust him," he whispered, locking eyes with Riley.

"What are you talking about?" she frowned, studying his leery expression.

"We've got two groups coming after us right now," he began, as if she needed reminding. "Your old boyfriend showing up outta nowhere doesn't seem suspicious to you?"

"You're the one who fucked around with the flashlight," Riley raised her eyebrows at him before gazing up at the ceiling. "Look, I get that it feels too good to be true, but I know Calvin. I trust him. And I really don't wanna be the one doing all the talking with those two sisters tomorrow."

"You trust him, but he doesn't trust us," Jesse replied as he pulled the sheets up to his chin, still trying to shake off the chill from outside, "Because if he did, he would've left his backpack in here with us."

"What difference does that make?" she narrowed her eyes as she looked back at him, "We both brought our bags out with us during the first watch. You haven't been out scavenging as much as me, Keith and Sterling… No matter how much you trust a person, if you get caught without your pack, you're not gonna last for too long out here. Think about it. If we got separated – someone starts shooting, a fire breaks out, the roof falls in, whatever – that's your supplies gone. So Calvin taking his backpack with him – that's not suspicious. That's smart."

"Or maybe it's paranoia that I'm gonna go through his pack," he countered with a shrug.

"Were you?" Riley propped herself up on her elbow to face him.

"It'd help to know if he was carrying a walkie or not," Jesse muttered, avoiding the weight of her stare.

"Then why don't you go out there and ask him?" she cocked her head to one side, waiting for him to make eye contact again. "Say, hey, Calvin, thanks for offering to stick your neck out for us tomorrow. I know you and Riley went to high school together, but I still don't trust you. Do you mind if I tip your bag upside down and go through all your shit while you're freezing your ass off standing guard for us?"

"Maybe you're right," Jesse replied, his stubborn tone switching over to sarcasm instead. "Maybe good things still happen in the world. Maybe we can chalk up this chance encounter to a happy coincidence, and your old boyfriend is gonna solve all of our problems tomorrow."

"What is this about, Jesse, really?" she sat up, challenging him. "You walked in here complaining that you were about to fall asleep, but now all you wanna do is stay up and talk shit about Calvin?"

"I'm sorry, Riley, but I just don't trust him," he shook his head in earnest. "This guy drops in outta nowhere, and you're what – you're just gonna pretend like the last six months on the road didn't completely fuck him up? You saw how bad I got after my mom died. Who knows how he's been dealing with the death of his parents? Who knows what he's had to do to survive? I mean, maybe you're not thinking straight because you said you guys were dating... But we've been together ever since the shit hit the fan, and –"

"You're jealous, is that it?" Riley asked the question that had been on her mind ever since Jesse started being such a dick at dinner. "We practically grew up together when we were kids, and after Hayden died, you've been the only guy at the end of the world that's around my age. And now Calvin shows up, and you're bringing up every reason for me not to trust him... Can I ask you something – do you think we're in a fucking love triangle?"

Romance was the last thing on Riley's mind, but she had to make sure that he wasn't getting any ideas.

Now, more than ever, she had to be careful around men.

She didn't want to end up like her mother – pregnant in the apocalypse.

"No, I never thought that," Jesse withdrew, his gaze sliding sideways.

"Good," she threw aside her tablecloth blankets and rose to her feet, "Because there's no chance of anything happening between anyone here. Not unless you two wanna hook up in the storage closet. But when it comes to me, as far as either of you should be concerned – which you really fucking shouldn't – I've got a bigger set of balls than the both of you."

With that, Riley snatched up her backpack and punched the service door open.

The freezing breath of the winter night soothed the frustration on her face, but she ducked into one of the bathrooms before the cold could take hold.

Flicking on Jesse's flashlight, she glanced around at the sink and stalls.

The bathroom was surprisingly cleaner than she had anticipated, given the state of the rest of the clubhouse. Even the mirrors were still intact, apart from a fine layer of dust.

I guess even vandals don't want broken glass where they shit, she supposed, grateful for the room's ventilation.

Riley set the torch down beside the basin, gazing at her dimly lit reflection in the mirror as she took off her gloves. Pulling out her black hair tie and shaking her greasy light brown ponytail loose, she began combing through knots and tangles with her scarred fingers.

Deep down, she knew that Jesse was right to be suspicious of Calvin.

But even so, she didn't want to believe that Calvin was anything other than the guy she had known back in Redhurst. The memory of his roguish grin after graduation – when he had first asked her out, just the two of them – was something that she didn't want to taint by sharing in Jesse's doubt.

Keep your guard up, a voice spoke into her ear, so clearly that she whirled around.

Pulse racing, she checked to make sure that she was still alone in the empty bathroom before turning back to the mirror again.

Brushing her hair back and tying it off into another ponytail, she remembered the instruction that her father had repeated over and over again while giving her lessons in self defense.

Keep your guard up, the echo of Nolan Armstrong reminded

her.

Riley could have called Calvin's sudden reappearance a coincidence, but she knew that hearing her father's voice again – now, of all times – wasn't just by chance.

Pulling her gloves back on, she hardened her gaze at her reflection in the mirror, resolving to check Calvin's backpack herself.

At least the request would sound better if it came from her.

Flicking off the flashlight, she left the bathroom in search of Calvin.

Riley took two steps into the clubhouse's moonlit function room, when a dark figure shot out from behind the corner bar.

She only had a split second to register the mottled white and gray of a winter camouflage uniform, before a rifle butt knocked her unconscious.

CHAPTER 20

"You're not going anywhere," the ghost of Nolan Armstrong declared, taking a step towards his daughter in the hallway of their house in Redhurst. "Whatever plans you've made, cancel them."

Riley's teeth were chattering, a vibrating tremor shaking her from the dream.

Flashes of morning light flared across her retinas as she blinked herself awake.

Slumped against the window of an idling bus with a pair of sore arms and a throbbing headache, she blearily stared around at her surroundings.

Soldiers in winter camouflage uniforms were hauling big red barrels out of a cavernous wooden barn, heaving them towards the side of the bus. The uniformed men and women disappeared out of view as they stooped to load up the diesel drums into the luggage compartment below.

The horse farm, Riley realized, sitting up in her seat, only for her stretched arms to jerk against a pair of restraints with a metallic jingle.

The bus seat beside her had been dismantled, leaving only

the undercarriage's jumble of railing behind, to which she was handcuffed.

"Fucking bitch," a husky voice seethed through her thoughts as a fiery red-haired girl was escorted up the aisle by a surly-looking soldier. Heather glared down at Riley, "I'm glad they got you too."

With her hands bound behind her back, Heather turned and kicked at the crooks of Riley's shackled arms, making her fold over the twist of railing she was cuffed to.

Sluggishly jerking herself back upright, Riley caught a fleeting glimpse of Heather's knee flying past her face, the escorting soldier shoving the girl off balance as he pushed her towards another seat three rows up.

"Hey, you're awake," Jesse called from the other side of the aisle, similarly secured.

He had an annoyingly smug smile on his thin face.

"What the hell's going on?" Riley sat sideways in her seat, watching Heather curse the soldier as he roughly cuffed her swollen wrist to the adjacent tangle of scrap metal.

"Your boyfriend sold us out," Jesse nodded towards something outside her window.

In the distance, sipping from the lid of a steaming thermos on the veranda of the caretaker's lodge, Calvin Fisher was idly chatting with a pair of grunts on guard duty.

"You fucking asshole," she narrowed her eyes at Calvin, feeling her blood boiling at the sight of his roguish grin, the trio chuckling at some infuriating joke.

"I hate to say it, but –"

"Then don't," Riley snapped as she glared back at Jesse. "I might be handcuffed, but that doesn't mean I can't kick your stupid fucking face through the window."

"You keep your shitter in your seat," the surly soldier warned as he marched back down the aisle, eyeing her restraints. "Any trouble and we'll strip your rat-ass and leave you for the wolves. Fuck around and find out."

She glowered up at the man's rigid stare, rattling her shackles against the railing in resentment. Her gaze dropped to his dog tags hanging over his winter camouflage uniform, reading *Trask* engraved on the stainless steel.

For a moment, she considered kicking him backwards over the mass of railing at his heels, hoping that he would fall right into Jesse's lap, where he could choke the man out with his elbow. If they took Trask's keys and weapons, they'd have a shot at escaping, while indebting Heather to help strike back at their common enemy.

The only problem with Riley's plan was having to rely on Jesse.

Unwilling to risk getting caught in the cold without her gear, and knowing that the surrounding suburbs had probably been picked clean between the scavengers and the soldiers anyway, she turned her attention towards another pair of prisoners being shoved around the side of the bus.

Taking Riley's seething silence as her submission, Trask strode on down the aisle, warily watching them from the front section of the bus as four more people climbed aboard.

"Hey, Piss Beard, put me next to my son," Keith Bowman spoke over his shoulder, his whiskey-cured growl contending with the rumble of the idling engine.

Despite the purple bruise across his stubbled jaw, the former policeman still managed to shoot half a grin back at the burly blonde-bearded grunt escorting him.

"You're lucky Turnbull wants fighters," the soldier named

Wheeler grumbled as he wrangled Keith into a seat three rows down from Jesse. "If it was up to me, I would've staked your ass out in the snow until the sun came up."

"That's why you're still a private, Piss Beard," Keith replied as he settled into his seat, his eyebrows raised in mockery.

"You know that name's sticking," Riley chuckled, catching a smirk from a Latina soldier passing by as she escorted the fifth prisoner – a wiry black youth – to the seat opposite from Heather.

"Dad, are you okay?" Jesse leaned out of his chair as far as his shackles would allow.

"I'm fine," Keith eyed Wheeler for a moment longer before turning to his son. "I've been to rub-and-tugs that beat harder than these weekend warrior wannabes."

"Dwayne, stop struggling," Heather exhaled behind them, watching with waning interest while her friend resisted the soldier's attempts to cuff him to another dismantled seat's undercarriage.

"Not until they tell us what the fuck they want!!" Dwayne yelled, spitting into the soldier's face.

The Latina woman pinned the prisoner's wrists to the edge of his seat as she turned away, her face twisted in stunned disgust as she blinked through his spray of saliva.

In a heartbeat, Trask's tan-colored combat boots thundered up the aisle.

Dwayne barely had enough time to stutter out an apology before the back of his skull was slammed hard against the window.

He was unconscious by the second battering ram to his face.

Heather's husky threats did nothing to deter Trask's heavy-handed punches.

It took three more brutal blows before the other two soldiers finally intervened.

Riley stared over her shoulder at Dwayne, blood-tinged strings of saliva drooling from his slack mouth as his head dangled over his chest.

She glared up at Trask.

"You're a big tough guy, –"

"Riley," Keith cut her off before she could finish her sentence. He shook his head gravely, cautioning her against provoking this particular grunt.

"Are you fucking serious!?" Heather craned her neck as the Latina soldier finished cuffing Dwayne. "Is he even alive?"

Wiping her face clean on her camo-print sleeve, the woman checked the prisoner's pulse before glancing back at Heather, giving her a terse nod.

"He fucked around," Trask turned back to face the others, "He found out."

"I guess we know where the military was when the world went to shit," Riley supposed, ignoring Keith's warning as she stared up at the surly soldier. "They were hiding on a fucking horse farm beating up prisoners."

"You don't know what you're talking about," Trask snarled, brushing off Wheeler's steadying hand as he advanced towards her next. "You don't know half the shit men like me have done for this country."

"No, I don't," Riley admitted, her head cocking to one side. "So tell me – where were you when people were killing each other in the streets? Where were you when refugees were getting ambushed on the freeways? Where were you when entire towns were getting slaughtered by raiders? Whatever you've done for this country, I don't know shit about it, because all I've seen you do is snatch and smash people who were just trying to survive."

"*People*," he chuckled, glancing sidelong at Wheeler in amusement. "All the good people are gone. Only the rats are left now."

"You mean scavengers," Heather bristled behind him.

"There's no difference," the surly soldier replied with his warped worldview. "Rats steal, rats run, and rats hide. Same as you. Only the ones that can be trained are worth saving. The rest are just an infestation to be exterminated."

"You wanna train us?" Jesse snorted in derision as Trask drew up alongside him. "What makes you think we'd do anything for you diesel-hoarding dickheads?"

"I'll give you one good reason," the iron-hearted soldier menaced over Jesse, a grim smile spreading across his face as he cocked back a fist. "I'm just getting warmed up."

"Well, cool the fuck down then!" Keith barked, wrenching at his restraints. "Because the last guy who put his hands on my son – I stomped his face in before we jammed a needle full of meth through his fucking eyeball!"

Fuck it, Riley thought to herself, sliding to the edge of her seat to take down Trask as he whirled towards Keith instead.

Just as she was about to kick the brute's caps out of his knees, the other two soldiers scraped and stomped their combat boots on the bus floor, standing at attention as a hulking woman climbed aboard the bus.

"Sergeant Turnbull," the Latina grunt saluted the oxlike officer, "Everyone secure and ready for transport."

"I can see that, Rodriguez," the butch woman's stern gaze traced over the fresh cuts and welts across Dwayne's face. "Trask, was that you?"

"Just handing out some sedatives, Sarge," the surly soldier straightened up in the aisle.

"There are better ways to use our resources," the hulking sergeant chided him, placing her masculine hands on her robust hips. "Go give Newman's team a hand. I want us outta here in five."

"Yes ma'am," Trask swelled with purpose as he exited the bus, whipping the other grunts outside into gear.

"He's a good soldier," Turnbull remarked by way of apology, her gaze switching from Dwayne to Heather.

"Did I ask?" Heather pretended to ponder, glancing around at the other prisoners. "No, I don't think I did. I do have one question though – what the fuck do you want from us?"

"As survivors of The Fall," Sergeant Turnbull addressed them all, "You are to be fed, situated, and put to work. We're packing up our supply depots and heading back to base in Colorado for the winter. You're welcome."

"*Welcome?*" Riley echoed incredulously, "For what? You kidnapped us and threw us onto a bus. We didn't ask you for help. We were getting by just fine on our own. Who the fuck are you t–"

A strip of cloth flashed over her eyes and pulled tight across her mouth.

Wheeler wrapped the gag's ends once, twice, and three times around her head before tying it off into a firm knot.

"You might not agree with how we carry out our orders," Turnbull marched up the aisle, eyeing each of the prisoners in turn before leveling her stern gaze at Riley. "But strictly speaking, we don't give a fuck."

CHAPTER 21

Night had already fallen by the time they saw an array of lights in the distance, glimpsing a tall grid of man-made stars through the bare-branched trees lining the icy riverside.

Ever since people had begun killing each other over resources, Riley Armstrong had thought that she would never see another house so dauntlessly displaying its access to electricity, let alone an entire building.

A flurry of snow borne on the frosty breeze buffeted the bus windows, momentarily obscuring the unfamiliar sight.

Passing by an abandoned cluster of motel rooms on the dark side of the river, the black and white tour bus swung right at an intersection, where a set of spotlights glared at them from the far side of a bridge.

They slowed to a crawl as sentries manning the military blockade waved them down.

Rumbling to a stop before the overlapping rows of piled rubble and stacked sandbags, the bus driver opened up the door, with its *hiss* and *pop* sounding above the idling engine.

Tan-colored combat boots crunched across the snow-covered asphalt, and a pair of guards boarded to check

Sergeant Turnbull's credentials.

Still gagged by the strip of cloth wrapped around the lower half of her face, Riley glanced around at the other prisoners, their mouths similarly muzzled.

Heather and Dwayne scowled back at her, the latter's gag stained with dried blood.

Jesse Bowman was staring out the window, gazing up in awe at the chateau on the other side of the river, its light in the darkness like a glowing beacon of salvation from the shivering winter's night.

Even Keith was placated by the idea that a working military had established a safe zone for survivors to seek refuge. Maybe the army had been here from the very beginning, and it had taken the soldiers six months to widen their search radius far enough to find them.

Riley didn't trust it though.

Not after Shepherd's cult community in Lake Springworth.

Not after Calvin Fisher had sold them out last night.

And certainly not while she was gagged and handcuffed to a bus seat's undercarriage.

She drilled her gaze into the back of Calvin's head as he sat up front behind the bus driver, waiting to see if he had the nerve to finally glance back and look her in the eye.

The pair of sentries stepped off the tour bus and waved them on through, the driver expertly snaking the long vehicle past the blockade before swinging left to follow the road's S-bend towards the chateau.

An identical black and white tour bus stood idling outside the entrance of a sprawling lot ringed by construction fencing, adjacent to the chateau. Passengers were alighting to line up outside a portable office shed, while soldiers marched back and forth, either patrolling the perimeter or unloading supplies from the luggage compartment.

One blonde woman fell to her knees on the snow-covered ground, sobbing and smiling in the glow of the floodlights illuminating the former construction site. A man in a hunting jacket stood by her side, offering a nod and a handshake to anyone passing by.

"Corporal Newman," Sergeant Turnbull summoned a short and stocky soldier to the front of the bus. "You're in charge while I check in with Drummond. Make sure they're fed and ready for briefing."

"Yes ma'am," Newman replied, signaling to the grunts sitting at the back. "Let's hope this batch is up to the task."

Riley watched as Keith and Jesse were led off the bus before her turn came.

A pair of rough hands untied the strip of cloth from around her mouth, and she took a begrudging breath, her eardrums popping as she was hauled to her feet.

Trask kept a firm grip on her upper arm as he shoved her towards the front of the bus.

If she had been paired up with any other soldier, she would have scorned Calvin for lying to her last night, but she didn't want to end up looking like Dwayne.

She felt the frigid winter wind cutting through her gray hoodie the moment they stepped off the bus. Trask led her around the front of the vehicle and into the sprawling snow-covered construction lot, their breaths misting in the light of the flood lamps.

"Hey, Trask, give us a hand over here!" Wheeler called from the side of the bus, standing beside a diesel drum that was too heavy to carry by himself.

"One thing at a time, dickhead," the surly soldier muttered under his breath. Keys jingled as he unlocked Riley's handcuffs, and he spun her around. "Listen up, rat. You scamper your worthless ass over to that site office, and they'll give you a new nest to shit in. You fuck around here though, there's no second chances. You're out."

Riley glanced over her shoulder at the line of refugees queuing up outside the construction site's portable office shed.

"I had a backpack," she replied as she rubbed at the raw rings around her wrists.

"*Had*," he echoed with a snort of amusement before turning to help Wheeler unload the supplies.

She seethed in silence as another black and white tour bus arrived, with more survivors streaming towards the construction site. None of them appeared to be wearing handcuffs, but they weren't wearing backpacks either.

Whatever this place was, the people weren't planning on traveling to any other destinations afterwards.

Riley scanned the growing queue of refugees for Keith and Jesse, but with everybody huddling together for warmth, she couldn't find either of them. Supposing that they were somewhere in the crowd, she joined the back of the line, mainly because she had spotted a crew of volunteers handing out warm blankets and cups of hot cocoa to all the new arrivals.

Several survivors flinched at their friendly approach, unnerved at the thought of being treated well by strangers for a change.

"Welcome to the Leadthorne Riverfront Hotel," one of the workers greeted the couple standing in front of Riley. He wrapped a blanket around the blonde woman before sizing up her companion in the hunting jacket, "Sir, if you wouldn't mind coming with me?"

"Sorry, they told us to wait in line," the nasally-voiced refugee faltered, shooting a sidelong glance at the young blonde woman beside him.

Riley caught a glimpse of the man's face, her eyes lingering on his broken nose that hadn't healed properly.

"It's fine," the volunteer reassured the couple, "The soldiers just have a favor to ask of some of the new arrivals. We'll process your paperwork afterwards."

The broken-nosed man leaned sideways out of the line, eyeing the queue of other men, women and children – the young and the old, the sick and the healthy.

"Oh, what the hell," he supposed with a shrug. "We already owe you our lives. I've been looking forward to pulling our weight."

"I'll wait for you wherever they put me," the blonde woman spoke in a small voice as her companion followed the volunteer. "See you soon, Halsey."

"What the fuck?" Riley grabbed the girl's arm, both women's pupils dilating in recognition. "Chelsea!?"

"Riley," Chelsea Preston jerked her hand away, resting it on her belly as her sweet soft tone turned into a sneer. "I guess they'll let in just about anyone."

"Yeah, just like Shepherd's cult, right?" Riley countered, remembering the shock and panic on the blonde college girl's face when they had decided to leave Chelsea and Katanya behind. "What happened – Lake Springworth didn't come as advertised?"

"You know exactly what happened," she fumed bitterly, her lips tightening. "Just try not to fuck this up for the rest of us while you're here. It's probably the only place left in the country that can help deliver my baby."

"You wouldn't have that problem if you hadn't –"

"Traveling alone, huh?" Chelsea cut her off, peering over Riley's shoulder at the new arrivals forming up behind them. "Or maybe everyone decided to leave you behind too. Poor you. I guess what goes around comes around."

Riley gave her a small snort as Chelsea turned back to the line, letting a few refugees fill up the space in between them.

She swallowed the lump in her throat as the former college girl's parting slap settled in.

Rubbing the back of her neck, Riley wondered whether it had been a mistake to leave her mother with Virge, Sterling and Abbie. Both women were pregnant, and they needed all the support that they could get. Even if they did manage to make it down to Texas without a hitch, Susan Armstrong would still be giving birth out in the wilderness.

And yet here Riley was, not in Redhurst or Whistler's Valley, waiting for a warm blanket and a cup of hot cocoa like the rest of the refugees who were eager for a handout.

"Hey, I'm glad you gave Trask the slip," Calvin's voice rattled Riley from her reflection. "I was just about to –"

"You fucking lied to me," she whirled on him, the anger of her self-loathing intensifying as she stared into his piercing blue eyes. "You said you were gonna help us, and then you turned us over to the soldiers. How could you? I trusted you."

"You're right, I lied," he admitted, running a thumb along his jaw line as he glanced at the other survivors in the queue listening in. "But I'm not sorry. If I told you the truth, you wouldn't have come with us. You're too stubborn, Riley."

"Fuck you, I'm not stubborn," she frowned back, waving off a volunteer carrying a bundle of blankets, only getting angrier as she realized that she was proving him right.

"See what I mean?" he replied with an infuriating flash of his roguish grin. "But I meant what I said about helping. You wanted to save Keith, right? Look at this place – weren't you all better off coming here, instead of getting into a shootout with a bunch of soldiers?"

"You made that decision without us though," Riley narrowed her eyes at him. "They knocked us out, took all our gear, and then cuffed and gagged us for the whole ride here. And do you even know what they call us? *Rats*, Calvin, fucking rats. How are we better off?"

"Just give it a chance, Riley," his piercing blues met her hazel gaze, "That's all I'm asking. This isn't a prison – if you wanna leave, you can. But I can promise you won't want to. All you have to do is play your cards right, and they'll take care of you. I'll admit, they expect you to earn your keep around here, but it's better than anything else that's out there."

Riley glanced back at the glowing chateau towering over the construction site.

There could be no doubt that the soldiers had stocked the hotel full of supplies and diesel for the generators. There would be running water from the river, along with the amenities in each room. And considering the military blockades guarding the perimeter – they were sure to have the best protection that the apocalypse had to offer.

Her shoulders began to relax as she felt her wrath relenting.

It certainly wasn't the destination that she'd had in mind, but she had to admit to herself – she sure wouldn't mind riding out the winter here.

"Okay, but still, fuck you for lying to me," she exhaled as she gave him a spiteful shove, harder than she had intended.

Calvin stumbled backwards over a rock hidden underneath the snow, and he lost his footing, landing flat on his ass.

He stared back up at her in wide-eyed surprise.

Riley's irritation dissipated with a chuckle, and she leaned down to help him back up, when a shadow fell across his face.

She stood upright, furrowing her eyebrows as a long plume of mist blew over her shoulder from behind.

"I told you what would happen if you fucked around," Trask's surly voice menaced in her ear.

CHAPTER 22

"It wasn't her fault," Calvin Fisher said earnestly as he rose to his feet, pleading with the iron-hearted soldier. "I was turning to walk away and I tripped over."

"Bullshit," Trask called him out on his lie "I saw you."

The queue of refugees shuffled away on either side, distancing themselves from the trouble. Even Chelsea Preston turned aside her sneer, the blonde girl balking at the thought that she might be punished simply for her former association.

"It was an accident," Riley felt the weight of everyone's stares on her. She rubbed the back of her neck, "I didn't mean to push him that hard."

"It's too late," the heavy-handed grunt seized her by the arm before she could even flinch. Hauling her towards the construction site's exit, he growled in her ear, "Whole world goes to shit, and you rats think consequences don't apply to you anymore."

Riley thought about thrusting her shoulder forward to break free of his grip, but there was no use – where would she run? Towards the street where they were heading anyway, or back towards the hotel that would block her from entering?

No – she would only end up making things worse for herself.

"Keith, Jesse!" she yelled over her shoulder to the crowd of onlookers.

She wouldn't have expected either of them to follow her – not if the hotel was as safe as Calvin had claimed it to be.

But at least they'd know what was happening to her.

"Your friends aren't gonna help you now," Trask snarled as their boots scraped over the snowy sidewalk. "Soon as those rodents start chewing the cheese, they won't give a shit about whether you're eating or not."

Riley dropped her weight and spread her feet wide apart, halting at the edge of the floodlights' reach.

The line of refugees in the construction lot looked away, resuming their huddled shuffle towards the site office.

"Can you do me a favor?" she cocked her head to one side at the surly soldier as he tried to shove her along. "If you're gonna walk me outta here, at least keep your fucking rat analogies to yourself."

"Trask!" Sergeant Turnbull shouted from across the yard, her tan-colored combat boots crunching over the snow. The hulking woman's long strides closed the distance between them. "I gave orders for our catch to be fed and ready for briefing."

"I thought you just wanted the males," he frowned, keeping a firm hold on Riley's arm.

"If I just wanted the males," Turnbull dropped her voice as she leaned towards Trask, eyeing him closely, "I would've said so. Get her prepped. I'll be there in five."

The butch woman marched towards the tour bus that they had rode in on, supervising the other soldiers still unloading the supplies. Losing her patience, she stooped into the luggage compartment and hefted a full-sized diesel drum over one of her thick shoulders.

"I guess there are second chances around here after all," Riley remarked as Trask begrudgingly hauled her past the line of refugees towards the hotel.

"Don't look so pleased with yourself," the surly soldier spoke out of the side of his mouth, "Dying cold, hungry and alone would've been better than what's waiting for you and your friends."

"What the hell's that supposed to mean?" she furrowed her eyebrows at him.

Trask neglected to give her an answer as they left the construction site.

Grimacing in his tight grip around her arm, Riley chose to follow his lead.

If Keith and Jesse were facing a dire fate, she wanted to know what they were up against before she took any action to break them both out.

The chateau's glowing windows lit the wide delivery laneway along the side of the hotel, where a group of grunts emerged from a loading bay, passing by Riley and Trask as they marched back towards the buses.

Riley's jaw dropped the moment they stepped inside the hotel's warehouse.

Rows of heavy-duty storage racks were stocked full, beyond any scavenger's dreams.

Lining the shelves were crates of hotel-branded toiletries and bed linen, boxes of batteries and candles, along with bags of seeds and clothes and other miscellaneous items. The shelves seemed to stretch on like a public library – and they were running out of space.

A handful of soldiers were supervising a crew of volunteers as they sorted and stacked the heap of incoming supplies onto wooden pallets. Workers used forklifts to place the loads onto the warehouse's upper shelves, while any food, water, fuel, medicine, firearms, tools and books were carted elsewhere.

Riley and Trask followed a wheelbarrow laden with gardening implements bound for the back door. Entering a whitewashed service corridor, the volunteer steering the tools trundled off in a different direction as Trask pulled Riley towards the nearest exit. The surly soldier kicked open one of the double doors, and a rush of warm air flooded her face.

Their boots drummed across the hardwood floor of the hotel's lobby, passing by a lounge furnished with sprawling armchairs. Ornate lamps cast dim yet stylish auras from corner tables onto the rich red carpet.

For a moment, Riley could picture hotel guests sitting in the lounge with their welcome drinks, asking for the Wi-Fi password or sharing stories about their travels with strangers. Eventually, a smiling bellhop pulling a laden luggage cart would announce that their rooms were ready.

Riley thought that she was still lost in her imagination when she caught sight of the steadily growing queues in front of the check-in counters.

"Room for three, please," a grimy-faced refugee hoarsely whispered to one of the receptionists, handing over a numbered card before clutching his wife and daughter close.

"Certainly, sir," the clerk replied, swapping his number for a key card. Handing it over the counter, she gestured towards another room off to the side, "We'll have your closet stocked within the hour. Please proceed to the hotel bar for a refreshment of your choice."

The man didn't trust the invitation at first.

His gaze slid sideways towards the other new arrivals milling about the bar in the next room. They were all swaddled in blankets, wolfing down olives and bowls of peanuts while sipping on nightcaps. One of the bartenders was sneaking glances at her supervisor before topping up any glass in reach.

The man's little girl ran towards the bar, excitedly asking for a milkshake.

"Go ahead, I'll catch up," he said in a choked voice, waving his wife after their daughter, before he broke down crying in the middle of the lobby.

"Is this place legit?" Riley stumbled as she turned to Trask, still unable to believe her eyes. "You guys kidnap people just so you can hand out shit for free?"

"Nothing comes free," the surly soldier growled as he pulled her along. "They'll all earn their keep – just like you're about to."

"Whatever," she shook her head, sick of not getting a straight answer. "Just take me to my friends."

"We're already here," he replied as they reached a row of frosted glass windows. Grabbing the door handle, he snorted in amusement before staring sidelong at her, "Just think, you could've been sipping drinks by the bar with the rest of them if you didn't fuck around outside."

With that, he threw open the door and shoved her into the room.

CHAPTER 23

Riley Armstrong was quick to catch her balance, her gloved palms shooting up to shoulder height like a pair of coiled vipers, ready to strike out at anybody who approached.

"There she is," Rodriguez chuckled, the Latina soldier gesturing towards the long black boardroom table dominating the center of the room. "Take a seat and chow down. Where's Turnbull?"

"Here in five," Trask answered, pushing past Riley as he joined the other grunts standing at the front of the room.

"Hey, I got you a plate," Jesse Bowman set down his cutlery on the table, pulling out a black leather chair beside him.

Riley lowered her arms as she looked around the room.

Keith and Jesse were sitting beside the door. Halsey was eating at the back corner of the boardroom table, with Heather and Dwayne on the other corner. And on the opposite side of the room, two barrel-chested skinheaded twins with face tattoos and short-sleeved shirts looked up from their empty plates to stare back at her.

At the sight of the steaming corned beef and rice waiting for her, Riley didn't waste another moment, sitting down beside

Jesse and snatching up a spoon.

"Any idea what we're in here for?" Jesse asked as she settled into her seat.

"I thought you guys would know more than me," she replied around a mouthful of corned beef, shooting a glance at the soldiers studying the back of a whiteboard.

"Only thing I know is they serve up some decent food," Keith shrugged, having trouble chewing with his swollen jaw. He lowered his whiskey-cured voice, leaning towards them both, "I think these guys are the real deal. You saw the setup out there. If they aren't with the army, then they're putting on a hell of an act."

"They kicked the shit outta you yesterday," Riley reminded him, peering past Jesse to study the purple bruise on his face. "Don't tell me you've already forgiven them."

"Well, it wasn't like I didn't have it coming," Keith chuckled to himself as he scooped up another spoonful. He locked eyes with some of the soldiers standing at the front of the room, "That boot-faced butch bitch sergeant sure is sensitive about her looks."

Trask glowered back at him, but Rodriguez cracked a smirk, tapping the surly soldier's shoulder with a pacifying shake of her head.

"I remember you three," Halsey's nasal voice rose up from the back corner of the room, the broken-nosed man glaring angrily at Riley. "You lured my brother into that fucking bushfire, and then you killed all my friends and burnt down our cabins. We've been living on the road ever since because of you fuckers."

"No shit?" Keith glanced sidelong at Riley and Jesse with a hint of pride. "Was this guy one of Shepherd's?" The former

119

police officer didn't need to hear their answer to know the truth. He turned his grin on Halsey like a man whose loud mouth had never gotten him in trouble before, "Hey, one-pump chump, tell me – when you were gagging on that fat sack of shit's limp shrimp dick, was your bulldozed nose whistling a tune for him?"

The ex-cultist sat simmering while everyone else cracked up chuckling, the pair of skinheaded twins on the other side of the table leading the laughter, their brassy roars reverberating around the room, drowning out Halsey's delayed attempt at a response.

"See? I told you," Heather elbowed Dwayne as she nodded towards Keith. "We got robbed by the fucking rhyming raiders."

"Don't tell me you guys know each other too," Rodriguez turned her gaze between the two groups.

"You could say that," Riley gave a small snort. "We broke into their house, stole half their shit, and I guess they got caught while they were out looking for us."

"Rats are stealing from each other now," Trask remarked to nobody in particular, not even surprised.

"I told you not to come after us," Riley locked eyes with Heather across the table.

"Oh, I never wanted to see you again," the fiery redhead bristled, straightening up in her chair and wincing at the pain in her swollen wrist. "It was my stupid fucking sis–"

"Shitty friend, Dwayne," the wiry black youth beside her finished her sentence, glancing warily at the soldiers. "I couldn't let it go, and I got us both caught. And now we're here."

Riley narrowed her eyes at them, wondering what had

120

happened to Taylor.

Heather returned her gaze, pupils dilating and lips tightening as she shook her head slightly, the expression on her face begging Riley not to say anything.

"Yeah, we're here, but what's all this about?" Jesse voiced the question that was on everybody's minds. "We've met these guys before – is this meant to be some kinda mediation? Are you making sure we can all work together before we're allowed into your community? That'd make sense, but I don't even recognize these two."

The pair of barrel-chested giants with face tattoos and short-sleeved shirts glanced at each other.

"They said, Vlad, eat, make friends," the twin with a hammer tattooed across his temple explained in a thick Russian accent. He shrugged, "Is good here. Everybody happy."

"They said, Vanya, we have job," his skinheaded brother added, a sickle tattooed on the other side of his face, "Vlad waiting, maybe eat your food."

Vanya lifted his plate to check the table underneath for any leftovers, and Vlad elbowed him in the stomach with a bark of booming laughter.

The entire boardroom shook as the two Russian giants chuckled and jostled between themselves, trading blows that would have broken a smaller man's ribs.

"So, what's the job?" Riley asked, furrowing her eyebrows at the wrestling twins before looking up at Rodriguez.

Before the Latina grunt could answer, the frosted glass door swung open, and Sergeant Turnbull marched in. All of the soldiers scraped and stomped their combat boots on the boardroom's carpet, standing at attention.

"Everyone fed?" the oxlike officer swept the room with

her stern gaze as Wheeler and Newman strode in behind her. Seeing that their plates were empty, she launched straight into the briefing, "By now, you've all seen what's on offer. This can be your new home. We've got hot water, fresh clothes and private quarters waiting for each and every one of you. But first, you need to prove your commitment to what we're working towards – getting this country back to the way that it was, or better."

"You still haven't told us what you want us to do," Dwayne impatiently pointed out, hoping to finally get an answer to his question that had gotten him knocked senseless for half the bus ride.

"All of you have been selected because you can hold your own," Sergeant Turnbull's eyes lingered on each of them as she looked around the room. "Surviving out on the road for six months – I can't imagine what you've all been through. But I can bet that you've picked up a thing or two along the way. You've become self-reliant, you know how to turn struggle into strength, and I don't doubt for a second that all of you have killed to protect what's yours. And that's why you're here."

"You want us to help you guard the blockades?" Keith surmised, taking the soldiers seriously now that they were about to get some clarity.

"Not the blockades," Turnbull replied, eyeing him closely, "But it will involve killing people who threaten our way of life here."

"You want us to kill people?" Halsey frowned, glancing at the others to check whether he had heard her correctly. "Aren't you the fucking army? Can't you do that yourselves?"

"Yeah, we could," Corporal Newman answered this time,

"Just like you could deliver that pregnant woman's baby by yourself."

Riley turned to see Halsey swallowing his outburst, thinking of Chelsea.

Sergeant Turnbull stared at the boardroom's row of frosted windows, watching the blurry shapes of other refugees shuffling past.

"We've all got jobs to do," the hulking woman continued, giving Newman a nod before addressing the others again. "The military has been kind enough to offer protection and comfort to everyone within our walls, but nothing comes free. We're rebuilding civilization here, and part of civilization demands that everybody else does their jobs too."

"What if we don't?" Riley asked, shrugging as she stared at the others around the table before looking up at Turnbull. "Like I said this morning – we were getting by just fine on our own. We don't need you, and we don't need to do your dirty work either. If civilization means killing people just so that we can survive on your terms, then fuck civilization. We're better off on our own."

"You think you could live off the land out here?" the butch sergeant placed her masculine hands on her robust hips, "Because without our help, and without your gear, the land is all you're gonna have left. We've stripped Colorado clean of any other resources. Remember, we found you in Kansas. That's how far we've had to widen our search radius for supplies. You're welcome to try though – see how far you can get on foot in the winter."

"We wouldn't be on foot," Jesse muttered in Riley's ear before glancing sidelong at Keith. "If you're serious, I could probably rig something up. We just need to go where they haven't been.

Somewhere their buses couldn't reach. There's no way they've cleaned out the whole state."

"Bet your life then," Newman shrugged, daring Riley and Jesse to throw weight behind their words. "The other option – the obvious option – is that you can eliminate the threat and earn yourselves a place among us for the winter."

"That threat's gonna be out there regardless," Rodriguez added, looking at each of them in turn. "It doesn't matter whether you want us on your side or not. You'll still have to deal with them, one way or the other."

"Just don't let them take you alive," Wheeler shuddered visibly at the thought, before grinning at Trask.

"So, who do we have to kill?" Heather leaned towards the other option – the easier option.

"Nobody you're gonna lose sleep over," Turnbull took two steps towards the whiteboard and flipped it over, revealing a map of Leadthorne's surrounding area. She indicated the hotel's position before tracing her finger along a lone highway, "There's a group of cannibals blocking our way west. They've moved around a lot in the past few months, snatching our people on supply runs, but we have reason to believe they're currently holed up in the Leadthorne High School. Captain Drummond wants us to nip this one in the bud before we get snowed in."

"Could you slow down for a second?" Riley cut through the sergeant's spell, buying some time to digest the information.

Her stomach turned, and she pushed aside her empty plate, the red streaks from the corned beef making her feel nauseous.

She hadn't even considered that some survivors had already turned to cannibalism. Sure, she knew what it felt like to be hungry, to the point that she was certain that her stomach was eating itself. But even on the road from Nebraska, when she and the others had struggled on the edge of starvation for three months straight, there had always been the reserve stockpile that they had set aside for Susan and Abbie.

But between the soldiers and scavengers of Colorado, if they had already picked the state clean, then for those people desperate enough to survive, there wasn't much of a choice.

Just like Riley didn't have much of a choice – Redhurst was still three states west, and there were no supplies left to scavenge.

"Okay," she finally relented with a sigh, before furrowing her eyebrows, "But I have to ask – why can't you do this yourselves? I mean, Halsey's right, you're the fucking army. Why are you asking us to do this?"

"The last squad we sent never came back," Sergeant Turnbull stared at Riley with her hardened gaze. "We can't let any more of our guns fall into the enemy's hands. But if the eight of you go in quietly, armed with knives, you might stand a chance."

"Knives against guns!?" Riley exclaimed, frowning at her incredulously, "Are you fucking serious? The only thing we'll stand a chance of is being their next fucking meal!"

"You broke into my house without firing a shot," Heather reminded her from across the table. "We were shooting to kill. Don't tell me you're scared now."

Riley exhaled her exasperation, narrowing her eyes at the redhead.

"Aren't you guys trained for stealth missions though?" Dwayne cocked an eyebrow at the soldiers. "You're asking civilians to do your fucking job for you."

"It's because you're expendable," Trask bore down on them all, planting his fists on the table. "We lose you – no big loss.

125

Less mouths to feed. We lose one of us – we lose a gun on the wall, we lose a dog in the fight, we lose someone who knows how to shut up, dig down, and follow fucking orders!!"

A hush fell over the room as the surly soldier stood upright again.

"Calm, little man," Vlad smiled, spreading his big hands. "I follow, is good."

"I like hotel," Vanya shrugged beside his brother. "We do job. We stay."

The Russian twins looked around the table, drawing begrudging nods of agreement from Heather, Dwayne and Halsey.

All eyes in the room settled on Riley, Keith and Jesse.

"I'll do it, on one condition," Keith sat up in his chair, his stubbled jaw set with stubborn determination. He cocked his head towards Jesse, "My son stays here. No bullshit. No jobs that put him in danger. He gets a free fucking ride, whether we come back or not. If you can agree to that – Officer Keith Bowman, at your service. If not, go fuck yourselves. I'll tell the cannibals you're sitting on enough food to last a lifetime. We'll come back, trash your shit, grab our gear, and be on our merry fucking way."

"Dad, we don't have to –"

Keith silenced Jesse with a stare.

The survivors and soldiers alike looked to Sergeant Turnbull, awaiting her decision.

"Done," she finally nodded, eyeing Keith before addressing them all again, "You'll be taking the long way around, so I suggest you get some shut-eye on the bus. And one word of advice – kill as many as you can before the sun comes up."

CHAPTER 24

The tour bus swung left, and Riley Armstrong almost fell sideways out of her seat.

With the full moon soaring high in the star-studded winter sky, and the snow-laden boughs of spruces, pines and firs crowding the valleys, the bus engine's gentle rumbling as they swayed with each turn had been enough to rock her to sleep.

But as her gloved fingertips brushed against the combat knife strapped to her thigh, she sat up wide awake again. Her joints popping as she stretched, she turned her head to the side to see that Keith Bowman was staring out the window across the aisle.

"I still can't believe you agreed to do this," Riley croaked as she blinked the sleep from her eyes. "Why would you leave Jesse behind?"

"It's a good deal," Keith shrugged, talking to her reflection in the window. "We do this shit for the soldiers, and we're home free – royal treatment in a five star hotel. I know I'd never be able to afford a place like that on my old fucking salary. And leaving Jesse back there, at least I know he's safe, just like every other time we've been on a run."

"I meant if he was with us," she dropped her voice to a whisper, eyeing the trio of grunts sitting in the rear, "We could've taken the bus. We've got weapons now. We could've rushed them and driven west until we ran outta gas."

"We don't know what's waiting for us back in Redhurst," he shook his head as he turned to face her. "We don't even know if we'd make it there alive."

"You're only saying that because they've got Jesse as a hostage now," she slumped back in her seat. "We don't have a choice anymore. We've gotta follow through."

"You know, the more I think about it," Keith stroked his stubbled jaw, hissing sharply as he touched his bruise. "The more I'm starting to like the idea of staying here. This whole time, the army's been working on getting the world back to normal. Why don't we stick around and give them a hand?"

"Are you hearing yourself right now?" Riley furrowed her eyebrows at him. "What part of being sent off to kill a bunch of cannibals with nothing but knives sounds like the world's getting back to normal?"

"It's all bullshit," Halsey's nasal voice called from a few seats over. "We were dead as soon as we signed up, and they knew it."

"Why didn't you say something then?" she cocked her head to one side at the ex-cultist. "You spoke up once and then you didn't say shit after."

"Same reason you left your boy back there," Halsey nodded towards Keith. "I got Chelsea and the baby to think about. No chance in hell that I'm gonna risk getting them kicked out, just because I was too chickenshit to man up."

"You know that's probably not even your kid, right?" Riley asked, glancing sidelong at Keith as they remembered the setup at Lake Springworth.

"Strong chance it is though," Halsey leaned up against his window with a wistful smile. "I gotta say, as much as you fucked us over back there, I really should be thanking you. After you fuckers left her behind, that girl was real grateful to me for looking after her. *Real* grateful."

"Yeah, well I hope it was fun while it lasted," Riley gave a small snort at the thought of Chelsea Preston shamelessly spreading her legs just to stay alive. "Because if you fight the same way as the rest of your friends did, I doubt you're ever gonna see her again."

"Quit acting like you're gonna come outta this any better," he replied, turning his dejected gaze out the window again. "If the army's too scared to deal with these fuckers by themselves, what chance do any of us have?"

"I fuck them all!" Vlad proclaimed happily from the front of the bus, the hammer tattoo on his face shining in the moonlight.

"And I shit throats!" Vanya declared behind the bus driver, the skinheaded giant carving his name into a window with his knife.

"You mean *slit*, right?" Heather asked behind them, dragging her thumbnail across the base of her neck. "Slit their throats?"

"No, I –" Vanya paused for a moment, grasping for the right words, "My English bad. I rip head. Then shit throat."

"Is beautiful death!" Vlad assured them all with a hearty grin, "Vanya English bad. But is good!"

The tension in the tour bus dissolved as everyone burst into laughter – even the soldiers sitting in the rear cracked up chuckling.

The pair of Russian twins glanced at each other uncertainly

before joining in anyway, roaring with delight.

"Alright, we're almost there," the bus driver announced as the engine started to slow. "I'm gonna drop you guys off just before that hill. Follow the road and you'll see the school on your right."

"Are you guys gonna pick us up after we're done?" Dwayne asked as they lurched to a stop, looking up at the driver's reflection in the big rearview mirror.

"We'll be here until sun-up," Corporal Newman answered from the backseat. "That's if you make it out alive. Be sure to announce yourselves and approach with your hands up, or we'll shoot you on sight."

"That's a weird way to say *thank you*," Riley seethed, giving the soldiers a sidelong glare as she rose to her feet with the others.

"Good luck," the bus driver gave them a solemn nod as they gathered at the front. He added with a sniff, "If you get cornered, don't let them take you alive."

A *hiss* and *pop* sounded above the idling engine as the door swung open, and the seven conscripts stepped off the bus.

The night was still, with the winter wind frozen mid flight.

It felt as though they were walking into a gigantic freezer, the frosty air misting and scalding with each burning breath.

Their boots broke through the layer of snow covering the road as they hiked up the rise in the highway, with the moon lighting their path once they left the beams of the bus's headlamps.

Gathering up her light brown ponytail, Riley pulled her hood up over her ears, tugging the drawstrings tight against the cold. She furrowed her eyebrows at Vlad and Vanya, the pair of Russian giants happily plodding up the hill in their short-sleeved shirts.

"You guys have a plan, right?" Heather dropped back to keep pace with Riley and Keith.

"These fuckers took down my whole community," Halsey said bitterly over his shoulder. "Yeah, they've got a plan."

"I need to see the entry points," Keith replied as they crested the hill. Following the curve of the highway, he added, "We'll be splitting our numbers though, just in case the other group gets pinned down. I'll take Riley and the twins. You three hit them from another angle. We'll meet up in the middle."

Riley knew why Keith wanted Vlad and Vanya on their team.

They couldn't trust the other three to watch their backs.

"So, we're the bait," Dwayne supposed, shaking his head in resentment. "We kick the fucking hornet's nest while you guys get the big meat shields to hide behind. Fuck this shit."

"Shut up," Heather bristled, shooting him a reproachful glare. "How many houses have you raided with people inside? None. These guys hit us in broad daylight and walked away without a scratch. Fucking listen if you wanna live."

"Keep it down," Riley whispered as she caught a glimpse of a parking lot beyond the trees in the distance. "Halsey, you take the lead. Watch out for any traps."

"Figured you'd pick me to go in front," the broken-nosed man gave her a resigned nod.

Leaving the road to creep through a thicket of evergreens, he snatched up a fallen branch and stabbed at the ground as he walked through the blanket of snow.

Measuring their steps, they slowly advanced in a single file towards the high school.

Encroaching on the car park, they stopped behind a tall spruce tree, gathering around its base to peer past its snow-laden branches.

The school's parking lot was ringed by a concrete retaining wall to keep the sloping landscape at bay, but it only offered a few inches of cover to hide behind. There was a small drop to the snow-covered concrete on the other side.

Apart from a few abandoned vehicles and a grid of defunct light poles dotting the car park, there was mostly empty space towards the main entrance of the school.

"Not here," Keith decided quickly, ducking back into the thicket of trees.

He took the branch from Halsey and prowled around the edge of the parking lot's perimeter, searching for a suitable angle of attack.

Shallow plumes of breath rose up into the towering ever-greens as they followed the former police officer's lead.

"We walk circle?" Vlad spoke in a low brassy voice over his shoulder, beginning to lose his patience at their slow progress.

"Close mouth," Vanya replied in his thick accent. "We follow."

They reached the corner of the car park, where a chain-linked fence sprouted up from the top of the concrete retaining wall, wrapping around a sports field that stretched on into the distance.

The drop from the retaining wall was much higher along here, and to add to their adversity, this was also the point where the thicket of trees began marching away from the school grounds.

Between the parking lot and the sports field, there was too much open space for them to risk being exposed.

They had ended up in an even worse position than before.

"I can see why they picked this place to set up shop," Keith grumbled, sucking his front teeth and looking up at the night sky.

"We've just gotta keep going," Riley nodded in the direction of the thicket's course. "We'll circle back to the other side of the school and find a way in there."

"Circle, circle, fucking circle," Vlad complained, one big hand on the corner of the chain-linked fence as he stared at the moonlit buildings. "I fuck them here."

"No, let's find another spot," Keith agreed with Riley, stabbing at the snowy ground with the branch as they continued behind the cover of the thicket.

"Come on, big guy," Heather urged, jerking her head towards the others. "Let's move."

GUVV!!

Vlad's mouth popped open, robbed of his breath, the skinheaded giant staggering just to stay upright. He peered down at his shirt, one of his big hands fingering at a flower of blood blooming from his chest.

CHAPTER 25

"Fuck, fuck, fuck," Riley Armstrong breathed as she watched Vlad keel over, the huge man tumbling down the side of the concrete retaining wall.

"YOU FUCKING MOTHERS!!" Vanya roared, the Russian brute bursting through the trees and leaping down into the parking lot. "I SHIT YOU ALL!!"

Another finger of hot lead woofed through the frosty night air as the sniper took aim at the barrel-chested beast charging across the car park.

"Are you just gonna stand there!?" Halsey elbowed Keith, before following the crazed giant into the snow-covered no-man's-land. "Vanya, run zigzags! I'm right behind you!"

"Stick to the fucking plan," Keith growled through gritted teeth. He whirled around and gripped Riley's shoulder, squeezing firmly, "We drop down here and split up after. That cock-juggling cum guzzler can't hit us all."

"Is he being serious?" Heather asked as she and Dwayne watched the former police officer jump down into the parking lot, hard on the heels of Halsey and Vanya. "It's knives against a fucking sniper rifle!"

Biting her bottom lip, Riley glanced over her shoulder at the thicket of trees, certain that there had to be a better way around.

But before she could will her legs in either direction, her father's voice rang loud in her ears.

"I'm serious," the ghost of Nolan Armstrong seized her wrist, swinging her arm towards the ledge. "From now on, you do exactly what I say, when I say it. Clear?"

"Fuck it, let's go," Riley stooped to grab the edge of the retaining wall with her gloved fingers, using it as a handhold as she swung her legs over the side. The parking lot's snowy surface crunched underneath her boots as she landed. "I hope you're right, Dad."

An explosion of concrete erupted from the wall, showering her in dusty fragments as she tripped over Vlad's corpse.

The sniper had her in his sights.

Adrenaline surging through her veins, Riley sprang up and dashed towards the car park's nearest light pole, before ducking and switching directions, a searing slug punching through the snow at her feet.

GUVV!! GUVV!! GUVV!!

Rapid fire rifle rounds whistled past as she sprinted and spun, ducked and weaved, stumbled and swerved across the parking lot.

Up ahead, she could see Keith, Halsey and Vanya creeping out from behind cover. Taking advantage of the sniper's distraction, they ran in equally erratic paths towards the muzzle flashes strobing from the school's second-story window on the corner of the building.

The shooter switched targets back to the three men, raining down hellfire from above.

Still starting and stopping, darting left and right, Riley spotted a dark red pickup truck parked along the side of the building.

With her heart pounding in her ears, she tore through the snow and turned, diving for cover behind the truck.

She hugged the concrete, the frosty air scorching her throat as she caught her breath.

Crawling underneath the truck's chassis, Riley listened to the barrage of bullets pinging off and punching through the panels of parked cars.

Keith's barked orders were drowned out by Vanya's roars of mad laughter.

Glass shattered from somewhere around the corner, and she couldn't tell whether it was one of the vehicles or if they had already breached the building.

So much for going in quiet, she thought to herself.

A flurry of footsteps scrunched across the snow behind her, and Riley instinctively reached for her handgun in the waistband of her jeans at the small of her back, her gloved fingertips scrabbling at nothing but the folds of her hoodie.

Remembering the combat knife strapped to her thigh, she pushed herself off the ground, knocking the back of her head against the truck's undercarriage as she drew her blade.

Spinning around in the small space, she held her knife out as a cloud of snow billowed underneath the chassis.

"You're one crazy bitch," Heather panted in her husky voice, pupils dilating as she stared wide-eyed at Riley's blade, mere inches from her face.

"Make room, make room," Dwayne landed beside Heather, promptly changing his tune as Riley turned her knife on him.

Breathing a sigh of relief, Riley turned back around to face the building.

The sniper was still busy peppering the parking lot in front of the school, but it wouldn't be long before the shooter's attention turned towards the other half of the intruders again.

Chancing a glance up at the strobing second-story window, Riley nodded at the other two before crawling out from underneath the truck.

Throwing their backs against the building's brick wall, they edged sideways towards the rear of the school, their shallow breaths misting into the night.

Around the corner was a dead end – or it may as well have been.

To their left was a storage shed leaning against the back of the building.

To their right was the open sports field, along with certain death by sniper.

And straight ahead was the tall fence of a basketball court, where they could get nailed halfway up by any other guards who were running towards the sound of the gunshots.

"Let's head back to the others," Heather suggested, already with her back against the brick wall again.

Riley paused for a moment, considering the height of the storage shed's roof.

If they could scale up the basketball court's fence to climb on top of the shed, they could shrink back to the wall and stay out of sight from any ground-level patrols.

Behind them, the sniper's shots died down with an ear-ringing silence.

She had to decide quickly, before the cannibalistic shooter started searching for them again.

"Maybe there's a way through here," Dwayne whispered to

the other two, pulling open one of the storage shed's double doors.

The snowy blanket covering the ground reflected enough moonlight for them to see a rear access door on the other side of the shed.

Navigating their way past the dark silhouettes of wheelbarrows, racks of tools and a ride-on mower, they tiptoed towards the back wall.

"Damn," Heather breathed as she shimmied past a workbench. "I just realized – we never checked any lawnmowers whenever we were out looking for gas."

Neither did we, Riley wanted to whisper back through the shadows, but being in the cannibals' backyard, she kept her mouth shut.

With one gloved fist clenching the hilt of her combat knife, Riley reached for the shed's rear door handle, slowly twisting it open.

Mentally preparing herself for whatever was waiting for them on the other side, she took a galvanizing breath to summon her resolve, when a blade pressed into her hoodie at the back of her neck.

CHAPTER 26

"Drop the fucking knife," Dwayne's hushed whisper menaced in Riley's ear, "Or I'll slash your spinal cord and leave you here. You'll be paralyzed from the neck down, so when the cannibals find you, all you'll be able to do is watch while they carve you up."

"You think that'd count as eating their vegetables?" Heather wondered, her husky voice sounding sinister in the shadowy storage shed.

"Fuck both of you," Riley snarled as she dropped her combat knife with a loud clatter.

Slowly, she placed her gloved hands behind her head in feigned submission, dropping to her knees before either of them could even think to ask.

She had to be smart though.

One wrong move and she was a prisoner trapped in the shell of her own body.

"Fuck you too," Dwayne replied, kicking her blade across the floor and out of reach. "We wouldn't have even been here if it wasn't for you."

"You got yourselves caught," she gave him a small snort as

one of her legs brushed up against his foot. "Don't blame me just because you couldn't dodge the soldiers."

"Yeah, that was our fault," Heather admitted, her footsteps drawing closer. "But we only got caught because we were out looking for Taylor, and that's because she went out looking for you. So don't act like you didn't have anything to do with it."

Riley leaned back, feeling Dwayne's knife pressed firmly against the fabric of her hood.

"Are you sure you're even gonna make it outta here alive?" she asked as the sounds of gunfire and shouting in the distance picked back up again. "Even if you survive the cannibals, what do you think Keith's gonna do when he sees my body? He was a cop before all this – he'll see straight through whatever bullshit story you come up with."

"You'll still be dead," Heather replied indifferently as she squatted beside Riley.

"Like it's even gonna matter whether he knows or not," Dwayne added, gripping her shoulder with his free hand. "This was a suicide mission from the start. Nobody's gonna question how the rest of you died."

Riley stared at the cobwebbed wall of the gloomy storage shed as if she was watching him through a mirror. The muscle memory from her father's training was just itching to twitch into action. In one fluid motion, she could duck her head down and twist her torso, deftly knocking Dwayne's knife arm aside and sweeping his legs out from underneath him.

Heather would be another problem once they were both on the ground, but that was a problem that Riley was looking forward to having.

She closed her eyes.

Dwayne drew in a sharp breath.

CRACK!

She couldn't move.

It was as if all of the air had been sucked out of the room.

Did he just cut my spinal cord!?

She dreaded the thought of snapped ligaments in the back of her neck.

Her ears were ringing.

Something brushed past her leg.

Then, the horrifying instant was over, and a new one began.

Dwayne flopped onto the floor beside her, with a bullet hole in between his eyes.

The shed's rear door creaked open as a pistol nosed its way into the gloom, a grim stranger appearing in the doorway, searching for his next victim.

The cannibal pointed his barrel at Riley, when Heather surged upwards, lunging for his arm and knocking the gun aside with her elbow, before plunging her blade into his neck.

Riley dropped to the floor just as a stray shot went off, the shed's walls ringing with the blast.

She strained her eyes in the shadows as she searched for her combat knife, when she remembered that Dwayne's blade was the one she had wanted.

Seizing the handle from his slackened grip, she sprang up to see Heather already holding her at gunpoint.

Gurgling on the ground, the cannibal was desperately trying to staunch the ebbing flow of blood pumping out from the gash across his throat. Meekly spluttering for air, his hands soon fell away, his entire body going limp.

"You need me," Riley pulled her hood back and stared past the pistol's barrel, looking Heather in the eye.

"What makes you so sure?" she asked, the gun quivering slightly in her hand.

"Let's see," Riley began, glancing pointedly at Dwayne, "Your friend's dead. You've got a shitty wrist. I bet that's not even your preferred arm. What are you gonna do when you run outta bullets?"

Heather exhaled shakily, her breath misting out through the crack in the shed's rear door.

"Mike, was that you?" another cannibal called from outside.

Riley's heart skipped a beat.

She locked eyes with Heather in the darkness.

"Abe wants all our guns up front," a second voice came. "Soldiers are trying us again."

"Mike!" the first man shouted impatiently before dropping his voice, "You think he finally topped himself? It's all he ever talks about."

"More food for us," the other cannibal chuckled. "I got dibs on his gun if he did."

Riley crouched beside the ride-on mower, while Heather backed herself into a corner, standing behind the rear doorway.

The pair of men tried to push the door open, but the bottom caught on their friend's dead body.

"Looks like I was right, cocksucker killed himself," the first voice grunted as he shouldered his way into the shed, stumbling over the dead man's legs. "Hold on – who the fuck's this?"

Riley's breath froze in her chest as the second silhouette squeezed into the shadowy storage shed, staring down at Dwayne's body. The dull sheen of the man's claw hammer gleamed in the gloom.

Heather's pistol rattled as she took aim.

"WATCH OUT!" one of the cannibals shouted.

Two shots went off in the flurry of movement, strobing the shed like a camera flash.

Bodies fell to the floor, and the gun skittered across the ground.

Riley exploded out from behind the mower, pouncing on the man with the hammer.

She shanked her combat knife into the back of his torso.

"Son of a bitch!" he growled as he whirled around, blindly swinging the blunt end of his claw hammer. "I'm gonna mash you into a fucking stew!"

Riley felt the wind whistle past her face as she dodged the attack.

Retreating a step for distance, she accidentally planted her boot heel on Dwayne's lifeless face, losing her balance as his head turned.

Falling backwards onto a workbench, she struggled to clamber upright again.

The cannibal was on her in a flash, ramming his body into her and raising his hammer for a death blow.

"Fuck – get off me!" Riley snarled, her pelvis pinned to the table's edge.

Icy adrenaline pumping through her veins, she flailed out with her free hand, catching his arm on its way down, and she began stabbing and slashing at his stomach with the knife.

Wet warmth splattered her hoodie as she thrust and churned the blade, its serrated edges pulverizing his entrails.

But despite his grunts of pain, the savage man kept on coming, tossing the claw hammer to his other hand, determined to take her down with him.

She let go of his free arm to block the blow, and he shoved her down onto the bench, leaning all of his weight into her chest.

Robbed of her breath, but still frantically carving up his stomach with her knife, Riley's eyes widened in fear, staring at his hammer as it worked its way past her frenzied defense.

"Don't waste your time," Heather's husky voice pierced through their growling grapple from behind. As casually as flicking off a light switch, she stabbed the man in the side of his neck. "Go for the throat. *And then cross him the fuck out.*"

With one sure sweep of her arm, the fiery redhead slashed the cannibal's neck open from ear to ear. Making his death even swifter, she grabbed a handful of his hair and wrenched his head backwards, showering Riley in his blood.

"Motherfucker," Riley panted, shoving the man's writhing body to the ground before wiping her sleeve across her face.

"Remind me again why I need you?" Heather chuckled, sheathing her blade to give Riley a hand.

"Fuck off, I had him," she knocked aside the offer, pushing herself up off the workbench.

"Sure," Heather spoke over her shoulder as she searched for the fallen gun among the bodies. "I'll admit – you make a hell of a distraction. Think we can be friends for now?"

"Just watch where you point that thing," Riley eyed her as she picked up the pistol.

CHAPTER 27

An explosion boomed from the other side of the school, shaking the building's windows as the two blood-spattered women emerged from the storage shed.

"Keith, I hope that's you," Riley Armstrong murmured under her breath.

With the full moon lighting their path, they crept stealthily around the side of a concrete courtyard, with the fenced-in basketball court occupying the center. The snow-covered walkway continued around the corner of the tall fence to the right, but Riley didn't trust all of the windows surrounding the yard.

They had to get out of the open.

"Let's try through here," Heather nodded at a mess of footprints streaming out from a pair of double doors on their left. "We're here to kill them, right? Let's go wherever they're coming from."

Clenching her combat knife at the ready, Riley curled her gloved fingers around one of the door handles.

Holding the gun with her good hand, Heather looked along the top of her pistol's barrel, staring intently at the widening gap as the door swung inwards with a slight groan.

A swirl of hot air flew out to greet them, the school's empty corridor illuminated by a handful of trashcan fires. Flickering orange flames danced with the shadows on the walls, wreathing rows of lockers and trophy cases in their hellish hues.

"Looks like my old school," Heather whispered, keeping watch while Riley softly shut the door behind them. "Feels creepy as fuck, knowing people eat people in here."

"At least it's warm," Riley breathed, shaking off the chill from outside.

Heather's boots squeaked across the floor as she started down the empty passage, and Riley grabbed her shoulder, easing her back to the entrance mat. Sharing a knowing glance, both girls began grinding out the snow from their heels before advancing down the lonely corridor.

They sidled along one wall, keeping to the shifting shadows as they drew closer to a pair of bathrooms, when a chorus of running footsteps drummed around the corner at the far end of the passage.

Hearts pounding in their throats, the two women ducked behind a defunct water fountain.

"Bree, get your ass out here!" one of the runners yelled as their figures flitted in and out of the firelight. "They blew up the truck, we're not going anywhere!"

"Shit, shit, shit!" a woman with a hatchet in her belt appeared in the doorway of a classroom halfway down the corridor. "I told you we should've run when we had the chance! What're we gonna do!?"

"We're gonna roast these sons of bitches for breakfast," the cannibal stopped beside the classroom as his companions scampered up a flight of stairs. "Grab the rest of our shit and meet us in the faculty lounge."

He turned to leave, when the woman snatched the scruff of his sweater, pulling him in for a rough kiss before shoving him away.

"Fucking animals," Riley muttered as the man's bounding footsteps faded up the stairs.

Steadily advancing down the corridor again, they passed by the closed doors of dark empty rooms, glancing through cold glass windows at the moonlit shapes of desks and chairs.

Skulking along a row of lockers, they crept closer towards the only classroom with a warm orange glow pooling out from its entrance, listening to the sounds of shuffling and rummaging emanating from within.

"You take her out," Heather urged quietly, hunkering down at the end of the row of lockers to watch the stairs. "I'll make sure nobody else comes through."

Riley nodded, taking a galvanizing breath as she tightened her grip on her combat knife.

Crouching down low, she peered past the doorway into the classroom.

Reams of black paper had been taped to the windows, absorbing the dancing light of a trashcan's fire in the center of the room. Around the bonfire, a mess of hastily-opened sleeping bags were strewn across the floor. And in the back corner of the room, a pile of broken tables and chairs were waiting to be chopped up and sorted into the stack of firewood beside the storage room's door.

"... made our choice," the cannibal with the hatchet in her belt muttered to herself as she swept out of the storage room with a backpack. "There's no going back now."

Pupils dilating, Riley ducked her head back out of sight, warily watching the woman as she crossed the classroom towards the teacher's desk, hurriedly stuffing supplies into her bag.

She had her back turned.

Riley slipped into the room.

Go for the throat, she reminded herself as she stealthily stepped between the sleeping bags, her eyes laser-focused on the back of the cannibal's neck.

Adrenaline flooding her veins, Riley lifted the combat knife as she approached the woman's back, poising to deliver a quick death, when someone else gasped from behind.

"BREE!!" a high-pitched shriek came from the storage room, and a second woman dropped a box full of batteries to the floor, "Help! Somebody help!!"

The cannibal whirled away from the teacher's desk, screeching at the sight of Riley's blood-smeared face and the crimson-colored combat knife in her hand.

Angry shouts rang down the stairs, and bullets began flying in the corridor.

Riley willed herself to move, but she was frozen by the sight of the woman's backpack lying open on the desk.

A can of pea soup etched itself into her retinas.

These people weren't cannibals.

The horrible realization threatened to engulf Riley and explode out of her throat simultaneously, when her intended victim seized the hatchet from her belt.

At the back of the classroom, the other woman ran to the pile of broken furniture, pulling a metal chair leg from the stack.

Riley's mouth dropped open, but it was too late for words.

Whoever these people were, they were going to kill her.

Bree swung the hatchet.

Riley's instincts took over.

Side-stepping away from the arc of death, she kicked the flaming trashcan across the room, sending up a spray of burning embers at the other woman.

Bree aimed for her neck.

Ducking under the axe head, Riley stabbed the woman's thigh, just above her knee.

She went down, but before Riley could finish the job, the second woman struck her from behind, caning her across the back with the metal chair leg.

Riley snarled in pain, the wind knocked out of her.

Twisting around, she elbowed the woman in the jaw, driving her into a daze that sent her stumbling backwards over the upended bonfire.

"Charlee, get up!" Bree screamed, staggering to her feet.

Riley narrowly dodged the next swing, backpedaling over the sleeping bags as the axe woman flew into a rage.

Limping around the classroom, Bree hacked and slashed at the air, grunting in agony and despair as Riley evaded each one of her attacks.

Charlee moaned in her stunned stupor, sluggishly patting away at the flames that had leapt onto her trousers.

"Riley, you good?" Heather called from the corridor as the gunfire died down.

"I got this," she wheezed, keeping her distance from Bree until she could get the air back into her lungs. "Save your bullets for the stairs."

Just as Riley finished her sentence, her legs went out from underneath her, and she fell to the floor.

Charlee's sober grin was the last thing she saw before the fabric of a sleeping bag came down over her face.

Writhing on the ground, suffocating in darkness, she could hear Bree's footsteps approaching, the axe woman's shoes stomping and dragging, stomping and dragging.

CHAPTER 28

"Breathe," the ghost of Nolan Armstrong grabbed Riley's face, his mouth grimly set.

"It's kinda hard to breathe with your –" her panting indignation was cut short as she remembered where she was.

Charlee had her pinned down on the classroom floor, the stench of the sweat-stained sleeping bag pervading her nostrils as Bree drew closer with the hatchet.

The axe woman's limping footsteps stopped, her grunts of exertion steadying as she stood above the bulging sleeping bag.

Icy adrenaline surging through her veins. Riley stabbed at the sleeping bag's layers with her combat knife, ripping a gaping hole through the fabric up to her face, just in time to see Bree's hatchet coming down on her head.

Rolling to one side, Riley lashed out at Charlee with the blade, slashing through the dense flesh in between the bones of her forearm, opening her up from elbow to wrist.

Bree's axe head sunk into the floor just as Charlee's blood-curdling scream reverberated around the classroom and out into the corridor. Both women reeled back in horror, their wide eyes fixated on her mangled arm.

Seizing advantage of their distracted shrieking, Riley sat up in the ruins of the sleeping bag, flipping the knife's blade downward in her gloved hand.

Lunging back towards Bree, she plunged the knife into the woman's neck, sinking the blade into the slender muscle just above her collarbone.

Rearing in pain, Bree tried to stagger backwards for distance, but the open wound in her thigh only caused her knees to buckle. With her shoulder out of action, two of her limbs were frozen in burning agony as she watched Riley wrench the hatchet from the floor.

"Please don't do this," the woman begged, holding up her other hand in submission. "Take it easy. Just – please, take it easy."

Riley cocked her head to one side for a moment, ignoring Charlee's screams behind her as she considered the possibility of sparing them both. After all, they didn't appear to be the cannibals that the soldiers had sent them to kill. They looked like two innocent girls who were just trying to get by.

But they were already too far gone.

Their chances of surviving were slim to none.

There were no ambulances on standby anymore. No doctors to call.

If they didn't die from the blood loss, then an infection would take them.

A quick death's all anyone can hope for these days, Heather's voice rang hollow in her ears.

Riley bit her bottom lip, before shaking her head.

"I'm sorry," she rose to her feet with the hatchet. "We thought you were someone else. I'll try to make it fast."

"What the hell's taking so long in there?" Heather called from the corridor, still watching the stairs. "Hurry up and put them outta their misery. We need to keep moving."

"You think you're about to give us mercy?" Bree stared up at Riley, as far as her bleeding neck would allow. "You did this to us. This is *murder*."

"You fucking crazy bitch!" Charlee screamed, grabbing hold of the hatchet with her good hand before kicking out the back of Riley's knees.

Riley twisted around with a snarl, her crisis of conscience vanishing as she wrestled back control of the axe.

Swinging the hatchet like a baseball bat into Bree's sternum, Riley yanked her combat knife out of the wheezing woman's neck before she could fall forward onto the floor, gasping for air as she bled out on her own axe.

Riley surged to her feet, shoving Charlee backwards into the row of blacked-out windows. With a guttural growl, she plunged her blade into the base of the woman's neck and slashed sideways, crossing her the fuck out.

A fresh spray of blood coated Riley's crimson face as she watched the woman gurgle in confusion.

Charlee lifted her maimed arm to her gushing throat, her disabled hand dangling uselessly. Her other hand searched for something to hold onto as she began to lose consciousness, and she tore a jagged column of black paper from the windows on her way down.

Riley stared at her blood-covered reflection in the glass, framed by the growing flames of the upended bonfire behind her. Hot coals smoldered across the floor between the scattered sleeping bags as she wiped her face on her sleeve.

Turning back to the teacher's desk, she plucked the can of

pea soup from Bree's backpack before leaving the burning classroom, tossing the tinned food to Heather.

"Fuck, Riley!" the fiery redhead dropped the can instantly, nursing her swollen wrist. "What – you wanna stop for a mid-raid snack?"

"They're not cannibals," Riley replied, eyeing the tangle of bullet-riddled bodies slumped on the stairs. "They had food. The soldiers lied to us."

"This doesn't mean shit," Heather angrily kicked the can of soup down the corridor. "Do you think if you started eating people, you'd lose your appetite for real food? Who knows, maybe pea soup is a good entree before a main course of boiled ass. How the fuck did you make it this long, Riley? It's kill or be killed out here. You need to stop trying to see the good in people. Everybody's just a bunch of animals hunting for their next meal."

"Just like rats, right?" Riley supposed bitterly as she crossed the corridor, searching the bodies at the bottom of the staircase for any firearms.

She hated the idea, but Heather was right.

Riley had been handing out far too many chances to other survivors, and it had only gotten her deeper into trouble.

If she had executed Heather and Taylor back in Kansas, they would have found the sisters' stash of fuel while cleaning out their supplies, and then Keith wouldn't have been caught by Turnbull's soldiers while they were out scouring for gas.

Calvin Fisher – her own classmate – had sold her and Jesse out to Turnbull, leading the soldiers to the golf course and landing Riley here, risking her life to slaughter a bunch of cannibals that she would have never even crossed paths with otherwise.

Even placing her trust in Dwayne to watch her back had almost gotten her killed.

That's why she was looking for a gun of her own now, to even the scales between her and Heather.

"Leave it," Heather mounted the staircase, training her pistol on the upper level as she led the way up the steps. "Soldiers will probably come through and clear this place out after we're done anyway. Let's not make their jobs any easier than we already are."

"Do you even know how many bullets you have left?" Riley grunted as she turned the last body over, only to find a knife that was smaller than hers.

"More than you," she whispered back with a smirk, crouching low as they rounded the corner and came up on the second level.

Craning their necks past the staircase's railing, they peered left and right in the stillness of the upper corridor.

Pale moonlight streamed in through the windows lining the empty passage, wreathing bulletin boards and locked classroom doors in a ghostly glow.

"You think we got everyone?" Heather wondered as they made their way towards the front of the school.

"I don't know," Riley kept a tight grip on her combat knife as she checked back over her shoulder, straining her ears for any sounds of movement. "Let's find that faculty lounge."

A burst of gunfire blared from around the corner, and the two women shrank to the wall, their pupils dilating at the flashes of light strobing from the next corridor.

CHAPTER 29

"Found you, motherfuckers!" Keith Bowman's whiskey-cured voice barked over the barrage of bullets blasting in the next corridor. "Cannibal pieces of shit! Oh, you're not going anywhere!!"

One high-pitched man screamed in agony as he collapsed in front of Riley and Heather, struggling to crawl around the corner with his kneecap blown out.

"Cannibals!?" the man moaned in distress, fixing his glasses before his wild eyes locked onto the two pairs of boots standing beside the wall. Quivering in fear, his panic-stricken gaze snapped up to see both bloodstained women staring back down at him. He threw up his hands in surrender, "Oh fuck, please! I'm a fucking pescatarian!!"

Keith rounded the corner with an assault rifle, jerking his gun barrel away from Riley and Heather before aiming down at the man blubbering on the floor.

"Maybe you should've prayed harder then, asshole," the vulgar veteran police officer growled before squeezing the trigger, blowing the man's brains out. His stony gaze went to Riley with relief. He looked her up and down, checking her over, "You girls good? Looks like you had more fun than we did."

"Yeah, I'm –"

"Riley, you gotta try this shit," Keith cut her off with an excited grin as he offered her the assault rifle. He called back over his shoulder, "Hey, Halsey, any left?"

"Yeah," Halsey's nasal voice came around the corner, before a final gunshot rang out. "Not anymore though."

"Pescatarianism isn't a religion – it's a diet," Heather said in a hollow voice, still staring down at the man lying dead on the floor. She turned to Riley, "Maybe you were right."

"What the fuck are you two mumbling about?" Keith peered down the corridor behind them, frowning at the cloud of black smoke billowing up from the staircase before turning back to the pair of women.

"I don't think they were cannibals," Riley swallowed the bile burbling in her gullet.

She thought back to every snippet of conversation that she had overheard between their victims, only now realizing just how badly she had misinterpreted their context.

"No, that's bullshit," Keith dismissed the idea, not wanting to think about the consequences if it was true. He flicked on the safety lever of his assault rifle, "Turnbull told us to go ape on a bunch of cannibals, so we went ape on a bunch of cannibals."

"But what if she lied?" Riley's mouth went dry.

"Are you hearing yourself right now?" he took her by the shoulder, squeezing as he studied the horror lining her blood-smeared face. "Why would the army send us to murder a bunch of innocent civilians? It doesn't add up."

"But they begged us to stop, Keith," she furrowed her eyebrows, her gaze turning downcast. "It was like they didn't

157

even know what they did wrong."

"And how many people begged these cannibals to stop?" Keith asked rhetorically before shaking his head. "No, these shit-packing dick-jacking itch-having bitches were just trying to get inside your head. Don't worry about it. Some suspects – you could grill them for hours, and even the detectives wouldn't know whether they were guilty for sure until the DNA tests came back from the lab."

"Even if we had a lab to test any evidence," Heather scowled, spurning the thought, "We didn't find shit. No bones. No leftovers... We did see a can of soup though." She shifted her weight, glancing back at the staircase shrouded with smoke. "What if these people were innocent?"

"Don't you put that shit on me," Keith growled, refusing to acknowledge the possibility. He blinked before going over to the window, raising a hand to his face. "Not now. Not after what we just... oh fuck – it's happening again. He's out there. Dumbass fucking kid. Stop staring at me!!"

He slammed his palm hard against the glass, the window shuddering violently.

Riley's heart sank.

She knew who he was talking about.

The ghost of the five-year-old boy from the worst night of his career.

Riley gave Heather a sidelong glance before joining Keith by the window.

She gazed out at the moonlit school grounds, knowing that somewhere in the snow, he could see the kid still staring back at him, standing in his monkey pajamas, holding his toy airplane, gazing up at the former policeman in wide-eyed accusation.

We can't change the shit that we're sinking in, Riley thought to herself. *The only thing we can do now is learn how to swim in it.*

"You're right," she conceded, speaking softly into Keith's ear before he had a full-blown breakdown. "It wouldn't make sense for Turnbull to send us after innocent civilians. Just because we didn't see anything wrong doesn't mean that it didn't happen."

"Well then, maybe we should check," Heather scoffed, hardly believing her ears at Riley's change of tune. "You think this place might have a kitchen? Let's start there."

"It wouldn't make a difference," Riley nodded towards the glimmering glow of orange flames creeping up the staircase. "You wanna go down there and look for some smoked ribs? I'm not gonna stop you."

"What'd you fuckers get up to?" Halsey chuckled aloud as he came around the corner, grinning at the thick black shroud of smog gathering in the corridor. Without waiting for an answer, he turned to leave, "Come on, there's another staircase we can take. We've done our job – now it's time to get paid."

"Yeah, let's move," Keith agreed in a choked voice, rubbing at his bloodshot eyes. "Fucking smoke's getting to me. Riley, let's go."

They jogged around the corner, nimbly stepping between the corpses clogging the corridor, dead hands eternally reaching for their fallen guns.

As much as Riley tried to avoid looking into the faculty lounge, she couldn't help but catch a gruesome glimpse of the macabre massacre inside.

Some of them had tried to put up a fight, dying with makeshift melee weapons in their hands, their bullet-riddled bodies draped over hastily-stacked furniture.

But most of them had died cowering behind cover.

Silently following Keith, Riley hoped that these people were the cannibals that they had been sent to kill – for both their sakes.

CHAPTER 30

Riley Armstrong stared out the bus window as the first few morning rays of winter sun crested the snow-laden valley, filtering through the frosty treetops lining the ridge.

Their ride back had been significantly shorter than the route that they had taken last night.

Across the icy river on their left was a modest row of inns, but even looking past their middling styles and sizes, the Leadthorne Riverfront Hotel was unmistakable, the chateau's grid of lights still blazing brightly in the darkness of the dawn.

Keith Bowman was sitting in the front passenger seat, making small talk with Halsey, in between long stony gazes at Vanya's final carvings in the window across the aisle.

With the school burning down behind them, the four survivors of the raid had swapped their war stories while walking back to the rendezvous with Corporal Newman and his grunts.

After their group had split up in the school's car park, Keith, Halsey and Vanya had lobbed snowballs at the sniper before breaching the front of the building. Quickly overpowering the guards on the ground floor, they had managed to reclaim the army's stolen arsenal – lost by the squad of soldiers who had gone before them.

Hungry for vengeance for his fallen brother, Vanya had charged headlong up the stairs to the second story, the Russian giant barging through bullets and barricades like a bear gone berserk.

By the time Keith and Halsey had reached the upper level – cautiously advancing in Vanya's wake – they could only catch a glimpse of the big brute's backside as he tackled the sniper through a window, his pair of grenade pins glinting among the shattered glass shards in the moonlight, moments before the explosion that had rocked the entire school.

As reckless as the act had been, Vanya had single-handedly crippled the cannibals' morale and won his vengeance for Vlad.

None of them could have imagined a more heroic death.

"Hey, we're here," Riley prodded Heather's shoulder from behind as the tour bus swung left onto the barricaded bridge.

"Already?" the red-haired girl stirred and stretched in her seat, her striking green eyes snapping towards the sentries as they flagged down the bus from the military blockade.

"Listen, if you need somebody to talk to about Dwayne," Riley began, trailing off as she saw a shadow cross Heather's face.

"What, are we supposed to be friends now?" she frowned back, twisting sideways in her seat. "Don't tell me you've already forgotten what we were gonna do to you in that shed back there."

"I never said we were friends, but we should stick together," Riley withdrew, returning her icy glare. She glanced pointedly out the window at Sergeant Turnbull approaching with the sentries. "The way I see it – better the bitch you know, than the bitch you don't."

"Huh, good call," Heather admitted, turning her spite on the oxlike officer instead as the bus door swung open with a *hiss* and *pop*. "But I don't need a shoulder to cry on over Dwayne. Before all this, he was just some kid from our neighborhood – a fucking annoying one too. He's not the first person I've lost, and he won't be the last. There's only one person I care about."

"Newman, report!" Turnbull's deep voice barked above the idling engine as the butch woman climbed aboard.

"Mission accomplished, Sarge," Corporal Newman and his grunts stood at attention in the back of the bus. "Threat eliminated. Nest's burning nicely, with only three casualties."

"Not the casualties I would've expected though," the hulking sergeant remarked, eyeing the bloodstained survivors before nodding. "Good work. We'll send up a scavenging crew after the smoke's cleared."

Turnbull held her position at the front of the bus, bracing her bulky legs as the driver expertly weaved the long vehicle through the bridge's barricades.

Swinging left, they followed the road's S-bend towards the sprawling lot ringed by construction fencing at the foot of the chateau.

When the survivors stepped off the bus this time though, there was no welcoming committee of smiling volunteers handing out warm blankets and cups of hot cocoa.

Instead, there were only a handful of bored-looking soldiers patrolling the snow-covered construction yard, their curious gazes lingering on the dried blood smeared across Riley's face.

"Looks like you owe me a beer," Wheeler elbowed Trask,

the burly blonde-bearded grunt jerking his head towards the remaining conscripts.

"Fucking rats, I should've known better," the surly soldier grumbled aloud as they crossed the yard. "No matter how many of them you kill, they always come back."

Riley narrowed her eyes at Trask in contempt, beginning to wish that she had hidden her combat knife before Newman's team had ordered them to surrender their weapons.

"Sign in at the site office," Sergeant Turnbull paused in the middle of the construction lot, gesturing towards the portable office shed. "After you get your new digs, clean yourselves up and report to the lobby. Drummond wants to see you."

Without waiting for their acknowledgment, the robust woman continued marching towards the hotel, the other soldiers falling in behind her without a backwards glance.

"Yes ma'am," Heather saluted sarcastically in their wake.

"You fuckers mind if I head in first?" Halsey asked, jerking his thumb towards the site office. "After the night we've had, I just wanna get back to Chelsea."

"Sure, go ahead," Keith replied, sucking his front teeth as he glanced up at the streaks of dawn in the winter sky. He clucked his tongue before looking back at Riley with a shrug, "Same shit for me, but for Jesse."

"You've got a way with words, Keith," she sassed him as he turned to follow Halsey.

"Hey," Heather nudged Riley as soon as the other two were out of earshot. "What was that shit you pulled back there?"

"What shit?" she asked, furrowing her eyebrows.

"*I don't think they're cannibals, Keith,*" Heather's husky voice took on a throatier tone as she mocked her, "*Oh wait, yes they are. Now, cheer up and tell us another rhyme.*"

"Oh, that," Riley turned away with a sheepish smile, just now realizing how annoyingly indecisive she must have seemed. "Look, what's done is done. I mean, it's not like we're gonna bring those people back to life anyway. I just figured – I'd sleep a hell of a lot better believing that they deserved to die."

"And I would've slept better if you hadn't brought it up in the first place," Heather kicked up a puff of snow as they turned towards the site office. Her plume of breath misted in the cold morning air as she sighed, "Something tells me this is gonna be a long winter."

"You planning on heading back to Kansas in the spring?" Riley asked, gladly seizing the opportunity for a change of topic.

"No, not Kansas," Heather spoke softly, checking around to make sure that there were no guards nearby. "I told Taylor if we ever got split up, the one of us that got away should load up the supplies and meet up at our cousin's house in Utah. We've got a good group, so she should be okay." The fiery redhead leaned closer to Riley, "But if anything happens to her – *anything* – I'm holding you responsible, bitch."

CHAPTER 31

Riley Armstrong climbed out of the hot shower for the third time in the past hour.

Maybe it was the miracle of having steamy running water again.

Maybe it was the tingling sensation of feeling clean for the first time in months.

Or maybe it was because she was paralyzed at the thought of having to pick something new to wear.

She stared down at the pile of bloodstained clothes bundled up in the corner of her very own luxury hotel suite.

The gray hoodie Nolan Armstrong had bought her when she was cold at the mall.

The pair of jeans she had worn since the day Grandma Eleanor burnt half of Nebraska.

They were more than just clothes.

They were memories.

Deciding that she would wash them herself later on, she crossed the room towards the closet, picking out something that would hide her half-starved figure, but also something that was practical.

Something that she could still fight in – if that was even necessary anymore.

Throwing on a double layer of black skivvies, a charcoal gray thermal vest and a pair of ski pants, Riley almost considered not going down to the lobby at all. She just wanted to surrender herself to the enticing invitation of her room's queen-size bed, sink underneath its thick blankets, and sleep for a week.

She willed herself over to the door though, knowing that the soldiers could just barge in, rip her from the bed and haul her outside. That was the price of relying on someone else to provide her with everything – at any moment, they could take it all away.

Slipping on her gloves and boots, she stepped out into the carpeted corridor, making her way towards the elevator hall. Feeling exposed as she waited in the wide empty hall, she stood in the corner beside a floor-to-ceiling mirror.

Her breath frosted against the glass as she kept her eyes on the corridor, flexing her gloved fingers.

Catching her freshly-showered reflection in the mirror, she could hardly recognize her own face. She brushed back her light brown hair, away from her peripheral vision, the cascading curtain smoothly draping over her shoulders.

My hair tie, she realized, just as the elevator's bell chimed.

The hotel staff at the reception desk had assured them all that their fight to survive was over now, but she wanted to be prepared for anything, just in case.

She turned to head back to her room, when she almost ran into Keith Bowman as he came striding around the corner.

"This place is fucked," he grunted, still wearing his fur-lined leather aviator jacket, with poorly-dabbed splotches of blood showing on the collar. "There's nothing but turtleneck sweaters in the closet. What am I – a fucking serial killer?" With a resigned sigh, he caught the waiting elevator before the doors could close. "Come on, let's go see whoever the hell's running this shit show."

"Did you see Jesse?" Riley asked as she followed him inside, doing without her hair tie.

"I caught him on his way out," Keith thumbed the button for the ground floor. "He said something about finding a job before all the good ones got taken."

The elevator jerked, and they instantly grabbed hold of the handrails.

"Gonna take a while before I get used to this," Riley exhaled shakily as they settled into the smooth descent.

"Could always take the stairs," Keith supposed with half a grin, before they both said in unison, "Fuck that."

Their boots drummed across the hardwood floor of the hotel's lobby, where they found Heather and Halsey sitting in a pair of sprawling armchairs in the lounge.

"Where is everyone?" Riley wondered, looking around the lobby for all the other survivors who had streamed in last night.

"I overheard a couple people looking for the ballroom," Heather shrugged, nodding back towards the elevators, "Second floor, apparently."

"Chelsea say anything to you?" Keith cocked an eyebrow at Halsey.

"We didn't do a whole lot of talking," the broken-nosed man shot him a wink.

Shaking their heads with a knowing smirk, Riley and Keith stepped onto the rich red carpet of the lounge, but before they

168

could sit down, another pair of boots marched towards them from across the lobby.

"Good, you're all here," Rodriguez said as she approached, "Captain Drummond's waiting for you outside."

"Lucky I dressed warm," Riley remarked, following the Latina soldier with the others. "Any idea what this is about?"

"Relax, he sees all the new arrivals," she replied, leading them past the hotel's buffet restaurant as chefs laid out platters of freshly-baked bread. "You guys weren't around for his speech last night, so he wanted to see you personally."

Riley barely heard a word of her answer, too distracted by the breakfast spread as they passed by the restaurant, her stomach rumbling at the mere scent of the sweet-smelling aromas wafting out into the corridor.

Rodriguez led them to an outdoor seating area, where a balcony overlooked the hotel's swimming pool, with a picturesque view of the snow-capped mountaintops in the distance. One of the hotel staff working behind the bar gave them a friendly wave, before realizing that they were only coming outside to see the captain.

Sitting at a square table in the corner of the balcony, underneath a glowing patio heater alongside Sergeant Turnbull, Captain Drummond was leaning back in his chair, taking in the views. He was a lean man in his fifties, sporting the beginnings of a red and gray speckled beard. His eyes were warm yet sharp in the shade of his old weather-worn army cap.

"Welcome," he stood to greet them, stepping out from behind the table to shake their hands. "Captain Wyatt Drummond. I heard you four had a hell of a night. I'd like to congratulate you on your victory, and offer my condolences for those who made the ultimate sacrifice – not just the three from last night, but for all those we've lost along the way, ever since this nightmare began."

He bowed his head in respectful silence, with Turnbull and Rodriguez following suit.

"Please, take a seat," he said after some time, gesturing towards the four empty chairs gathered around the table as he sat down between Turnbull and the balcony railing again. "I'll admit I was skeptical when Gretchen here suggested sending survivors to clear out the cannibals for us, but it came as a welcome surprise to hear that you succeeded where we failed. Anyone care for a coffee? Something stronger? You've earned it."

"No, I'm good," Riley declined as she sat down. She glanced at the silent stern gaze of Gretchen Turnbull, still not completely convinced of the soldiers' intentions.

"Hot water for me," Keith settled into the chair opposite Drummond. "Kicking coffee was hell last time. I'd rather not go through that shit again if we run out here."

"Don't jinx it," Heather narrowed her eyes at him from across the table, "I'll have a coffee."

"Well, shit, if you're offering," Halsey grinned as he sat in between Heather and Turnbull, already testing their limits, "Bottle of bourbon."

"Something from the top shelf," Drummond signaled to Rodriguez. "Bring back an extra glass for me."

"So, it's official," Keith supposed, kicking off the round of questions, "Government's finally taking back control of the country?"

"Officially, no," Drummond began with the patience of a man who had done this dance a countless number of times. "Back before comms went dark, we actually had orders to abandon our post at Fort Rushcliffe, and move all of our forces over to Boston."

"Looks like you missed a few turns," Heather couldn't help herself, earning an icy stare from Turnbull.

"We knew that asteroid was gonna plunge half the country into chaos," he continued, ignoring her remark, "But we weren't gonna let that happen here. So our entire company went AWOL under my command, and we chose this site for its strategic position, in addition to its ability to sustain a significant civilian population. The hotel's staff have been kind enough to accommodate us, along with all of you, until we can get back on our feet again."

"Wait, so that was it?" Riley furrowed her eyebrows as the bartender served their drinks. "Your orders were to go to Boston. You haven't heard anything else since?"

"Nothing," Sergeant Turnbull answered this time, breaking her silence. "Not since our own nukes came back down on us. Our long-range comms aren't working anymore, and after we separated from the rest of our battalion, we've effectively been cut off."

"That's weird," Halsey pondered as the bartender poured bourbon into his glass. "We were running a broadcast from a radio tower up in Nebraska, and that was working fine. But if you're talking from here to the East Coast, maybe it's all the radiation from those nukes that's scrambling the signals?"

"Disturbance from radiation would've only lasted for a few hours," Drummond replied, swirling his drink. "The only explanation I can think of is that there's somebody actively jamming our frequencies, and if that's the case, it's gonna take us a hell of a lot longer to get things back to normal."

"Have you sent anyone over to Boston?" Keith stroked his stubbled jaw, flinching slightly as he brushed his fading bruise. "Looks like you've got enough gas to make the trip."

"We're still looking for a way around the lingering radiation," the captain said solemnly before taking a sip of his bourbon, breathing out the burn. "We've sent scouts in every other direction, but it's the same story all over – country's full of desperate civilians just trying to survive. We're maintaining order in this region though, and that's good enough for most people."

"But nothing comes free," Turnbull reminded them all. "You'll still be expected to do your part if you wanna stay here."

"What, was last night not good enough?" Heather bristled, scowling at the sergeant.

"Last night gets you a pass for today," the butch woman replied, watching as Halsey polished off his drink and poured himself another glass. "Starting tomorrow, you'll each be assigned new jobs."

"What else needs to be done around here?" Riley wondered, cocking her head to one side. "I would've thought that between your soldiers and the hotel staff, you'd have every job covered."

"Not all of them," Drummond smiled, casting a glance at the snow-covered landscape beyond the icy river. "We've been here for six months now, and we still haven't received any news of an official initiative to help rebuild civilization – other than us. We have to assume that there's no help coming, so we're gonna have to help each other. The resources that we've stockpiled aren't gonna last forever, and we can't keep on scavenging."

"No shit," Keith squared his jaw, eyeing them both with his stony gaze. "What do you want us to do?"

"We need to become a self-contained settlement," Drummond looked at each of them in turn. "We need construction workers to strip the surrounding buildings to put up permanent fences. We need engineers, mechanics and electricians to rig up windmills and watermills. We need laborers to clear an area for farmland. Hunters, butchers, chefs, doctors, teachers, barbers – everyone has a skill to use and a role to play. One day, we'll all be able to live free and in abundance again, but until then, there are no more days off."

"So enjoy today," Sergeant Turnbull rose to her feet beside Drummond, "Because tomorrow, we're putting you to work."

CHAPTER 32

"I dunno about you fuckers," Halsey slurred as he stumbled back inside, already buzzing from the bottle of bourbon clutched in his hand, "But I could hunt and fish all day long. This is a damn vacation for me."

"Yeah, that's if they have any spots left for hunting and fishing," Riley gave him a small snort as she let the door to the balcony swing shut behind her. "With everybody else starting work today, we're gonna get stuck with all the shitty jobs that nobody else wanted."

"Is there a doctor around here?" Heather asked Rodriguez as the Latina soldier led them down the corridor towards the hotel's buffet restaurant. "I need to get my wrist checked out if I'm gonna be working my ass off."

"Sure, I'll take you there on my way to the gym," Rodriguez replied, striding back towards the lobby.

"There's a gym here?" Keith's boots carried him away from the restaurant as he caught up to the pair of women, his half-starved muscles eager to put some size back on his frame.

Riley shook her head in his wake as she and Halsey turned towards the restaurant. Cutlery clattered above groans of guilty pleasure, with dozens of other survivors already wolfing down the breakfast buffet.

Waiting for one of the hotel staff to notice them standing at the entrance, Riley gave Halsey a sidelong glance, unsure if she wanted to be seated at a table with just the tipsy ex-cultist for company. After all, only three months ago, she had broken his nose, lured his brother into a bushfire, and destroyed his little lakeside cult community.

And at the rate that he was drinking, it was only a matter of time before his bourbon would dredge up those same memories.

An elevator's bell chimed from around the corner, and a gaggle of voices soon filled the lobby, with the new arrivals excitedly chattering about getting back to working for a living again.

"I think I'm gonna head up to that ballroom," Halsey decided as another elevator dinged, taking a long swig from his bottle before swaying towards the oncoming crowd.

Riley breathed a small sigh of relief as she watched him stagger off.

Although now, she was standing alone in a hotel full of strangers.

"Table for one?" a waiter appeared behind the service counter, smiling at Riley as he held up his thumbs and forefingers in a rectangle, "Might I see your room's key card?"

"Sure," she reached over her shoulder for her backpack that was no longer there. Frowning for a moment, she patted the pockets of her charcoal gray thermal vest, before finding the key card in her ski pants. "It's not just me though. I'm waiting on some friends."

It was a lie.

Partly because she wanted them to know that people would be looking for her if she went missing.

But also because if this was indeed the rebirth of civilization, she didn't want to be seen as some sort of social pariah.

"Right this way, Miss Armstrong," the waiter gestured for her to follow him.

Passing between plush leather dining chairs and sleek hardwood tables, Riley's eyes widened at the sight of freshly-baked bread rolls and quiches, fruit spreads and cereals, fried eggs and steaming waffles, with jugs of juice and urns of coffee to wash it all down.

"This is your table," the waiter pulled out a chair for her by the window. "You're welcome to eat as much as you like, but please be mindful of leaving any leftovers. We don't want anything to go to waste."

"Are you kidding?" Riley tore her eyes from the bounty of food for a fleeting second, glancing back at him incredulously, "There's not gonna be any leftovers. I'm just gonna sit in here all day and eat myself sick!"

A sunken-eyed wafer-thin woman clucked her tongue in passing, looking Riley up and down as the waiter weaved his way back towards the front of the restaurant.

"You must be one of the new ones from last night," she supposed, holding her plate of a single bread roll and a stick of butter. "The only people who can sit around all day long doing nothing are the soldiers. Everybody else is just a pair of hands to be fed."

"And fed well, by the looks of it," Riley jerked her head towards the buffet counters.

"You're looking at all the wrong things," the woman smiled as she turned to leave.

"What the hell's that supposed to mean?" she furrowed her eyebrows, her impending raid on the all-you-can-eat breakfast buffet cut off by her own curiosity.

"Stick around long enough and you'll find out," the haggard woman answered cryptically, before making her way towards a lonely group of tables near the bathroom.

Riley swallowed, staring after her for a moment longer before her hunger took over.

Joining the queue of survivors lining up for the buffet counters, her mouth salivated at all of the sights and smells that – just yesterday – she couldn't have even imagined experiencing ever again.

Fresh eggs sizzled around onions and cheese and ham as omelets were made to order. Sweetly-spiced sausages and hash browns breathed life into the restaurant as bain-maries opened and shut. Chefs replaced platters of stuffed olives and sushi rolls just as quickly as they were being emptied.

One woman excused herself from the line, heaving grateful sobs while her husband ate with his hands to make more room on his plate, his starved eyes already devouring the next breakfast tray before he could even choke down the food in his mouth.

"Just when I thought this morning was perfect," a familiar tone moaned with an exaggerated sigh, "I get stuck standing behind you."

Riley turned back to see Chelsea Preston's sneering face feigning a sulk.

Giving the former college girl a small snort of amusement, Riley reached down to open up the nearest bain-marie.

"Here, let me get you some of this," she offered earnestly, seizing a pair of tongs and flipping a greasy rasher of bacon onto the blonde vegan's plate. "Extra protein for whoever's kid's growing inside your stomach."

Chelsea's mouth popped open in disgust, and she resentfully swapped plates with the man standing behind her.

"Keeping that diet must've been hard these past few months," Riley remarked, stifling her victorious smirk. "I still don't understand why you would wanna limit yourself like that, especially while there was so little choice out there on the road. I bet you made sure Halsey earned his nightly mounts – or maybe you didn't."

"How about you focus on keeping the line moving?" Chelsea scowled back as she dropped a hash brown onto her plate. "Sure, veganism has its drawbacks sometimes. But you'd be surprised at how much is on the menu when you don't have to kill for your food. And besides, it looks like I ate a whole lot better than you."

"Cut the shit, where's Katanya?" Riley craned her neck to gaze down the length of the growing queue, only earning herself the impatient ire of hungry glares.

"What makes you think I'd tell you?" Chelsea chirped out of the side of her mouth as they shuffled along. "It's not like you ever gave a shit about any of us anyway. Greg's gone. Shaun's gone. I don't know what the fuck happened to Hayden, but I'm pretty sure he's gone too."

"Yeah, he died trying to save you," Riley stared sidelong at her, the other people waiting in line behind them be damned. "Same as my grandma. Same as your own brother. And there you were, just one day later, living it up in that fucking cult community like you were on a fucking holiday. That's why we left you behind. Now tell me what happened to Katanya so that I never have to talk to you again."

"I have no idea," Chelsea wilted under her harsh glare. "She got kicked out before I even had a chance to talk some sense into her. Stupid. That deal from Shepherd and Quinn was the best thing that any of us girls could've hoped for, and she turned it down. Even this place isn't as good as we had it back there. And you just had to ruin it for the rest of us."

"You're lucky you're pregnant, bitch," Riley menaced before whirling away from the line with only half a plate of food, her appetite consumed with spite.

She sat at her table by the window, with a sinking feeling in her chest.

Ever since leaving Lake Springworth, Riley had resented Katanya for being as equally weak-minded as Chelsea, when she was probably still somewhere out there, struggling to survive in the wintry landscape of her own moral high ground.

Maybe things would have been different if Katanya hadn't been the first to get caught by Shepherd's men. They might have even held the farm against the cultists, considering the woman's skill with a hunting rifle.

Riley munched on a croissant as she ruminated on the endless possibilities that stemmed from the single *what-if*.

"Hey, sorry I didn't come by your room this morning," Jesse Bowman interrupted her thoughts as he sat down with an omelet waffle sandwich. "How'd last night go? I heard Dwayne and those Russian guys got killed. Were you hurt?"

"No, I'm good," Riley frowned for a moment, scarcely able to believe that only last night, she had taken part in a brutal bloody massacre, and now she was eating breakfast at a buffet restaurant in a five star hotel. She flipped the focus back on him before he could probe any further, "How was Career Day?"

"They're putting me and a couple other guys in the garage,"

he shrugged, taking a bite out of his sandwich, "Wherever that is."

"Car duty, huh?" Riley smirked at him around her mouthful of croissant. "I figured as much. You know, at this stage, I honestly can't imagine you doing anything else."

"Is that really all you see me as?" Jesse's shoulders slumped, stung by her words. "Just because I'm good with cars doesn't mean I'm bad at everything else. I would've been on that raid with you last night, if it hadn't been for my dad always holding me back. I'm sick of being pigeonholed all the time."

"Jesse, I didn't mean it like –"

"I hope I'm not interrupting anything," Calvin Fisher cut across Riley's attempt to smooth things over as he sat down beside her. He slid a slice of margarita pizza onto her plate with a flash of his roguish grin, "I noticed you didn't make it over to the pizza section."

"And I noticed you handed us over to the soldiers back in Kansas," Jesse turned his frustration towards him instead. "Find somewhere else to sit, asshole."

"Hey, I'm sorry about what happened," Calvin ran a thumb along his jaw line as he searched for the right words. "It's just – it's part of my job."

"Oh, so you're a professional asshole?" Jesse raised his eyebrows in mockery.

"No," Calvin chuckled at the insult he had walked into, glancing sidelong at Riley with a grin. "I'm a recruiter. My job is to bring people back here to help build up the settlement. So, when we ran into each other in Kansas, it wasn't by chance. I was there with the soldiers, hoping to recruit some more survivors."

"*Recruit?*" Riley echoed incredulously, sharing his smile,

"More like *kidnap*. But I've gotta admit – eating pizza and bacon for breakfast sure beats the hell outta those tuna crackers we were having back in that freezing clubhouse kitchen."

"They tasted good to me," Jesse bitterly set down his waffle sandwich and sat back in his chair, misinterpreting her meaning for the second time. "And just think – all you had to do to get here was risk your lives to kill a bunch of strangers for the people who kidnapped us."

"Yeah, about that," Calvin interjected, trying to ease the tension building at the table. He locked eyes with Riley, "I just wanna apologize – I never wanted you to go out on that raid. That's why I was trying to get you signed in last night, but then, well, you know what happened. But you survived, and you're here now, and that's what's important. Let's focus on that and be grateful."

Jesse fell silent in begrudging agreement, his sullen gaze glued to his plate.

Riley was still working on her gratitude, but the breakfast buffet was certainly helping.

"So, I was thinking," Calvin broke through the spell of silence that had fallen over the table, "Riley, maybe you'd feel more at home if your mom was here, along with the rest of your group that went down to Texas. Do you happen to know where they went in particular?"

Riley was about to tell him *Whistler's Valley*, when Jesse cleared his throat across the table, slowly shaking his head.

She furrowed her eyebrows at him before turning back to Calvin.

And that's when she saw it.

A hint of hunger in his piercing blue gaze.

It wasn't compassion in his eyes, but something else, almost like a subtle coax.

"We've got doctors and midwives available here," Calvin continued, leaning towards her with his boyish charm. "Your mom and that other woman you mentioned – Abbie – we'd be able to help them deliver their babies safe and sound."

"What about all the snow on the roads?" Riley asked, still watching him warily.

"Don't worry about it," he shrugged, glancing out the restaurant window at the snow-capped mountaintops in the distance. "There's still some time left for last-minute trips. I could jump on the next tour bus down to Texas, and we'd be on our way back with your mom and the rest of your friends by tomorrow night. All you have to do is tell me where they went."

CHAPTER 33

Riley Armstrong cut her rasher of bacon into bite-sized strips as she contemplated Calvin's offer.

It sounded reasonable enough.

There was no doubt in her mind that her mother and Abbie would be better off moving to the hotel. It sure beat delivering two babies out in the Texan wilderness of Whistler's Valley with just Virge and Sterling on hand.

But there was something about the yearning in Calvin's face that was putting her off.

She opened her mouth to reel off an excuse to buy herself some more time, when a pair of heavy boots approached from behind.

Keith Bowman dropped his laden plate onto the sleek hardwood table with a loud clatter, pulling up a chair with renewed vigor in his stony gaze.

"Where have you been?" Jesse looked at his father with a combination of curiosity and relief, before shooting a triumphant glance at Calvin.

"Went for a workout," Keith answered, before shoveling a spoonful of poached eggs and baked beans into his mouth. He locked eyes with Rodriguez across the restaurant as the Latina soldier queued up for the breakfast buffet. "My first time back in the gym since we left Redhurst. I didn't plan on overdoing it, but fuck did I miss those weights."

"I'll let you guys catch up," Calvin stood decidedly, picking up his untouched plate. He turned to Riley, "Some of the guys working in the hotel say there's still a few more days before winter really hits. Just let me know soon, otherwise we might be waiting until spring for the roads to clear up again."

Keith looked Calvin over with mild interest as he walked away, the former police officer sucking his front teeth before clucking his tongue.

"You sure move quick," he eyed Riley with a grin. "Shit, we just got here."

"Fuck you," she gave him a small snort, stabbing at a piece of bacon with her fork.

"I still don't trust him," Jesse said as he watched Calvin join another group of new arrivals. Seeing Riley bite her bottom lip, he changed the subject, "So, what kinda jobs did you guys get?"

"We don't know yet," she replied, popping the bacon into her mouth, her tongue salivating the moment the crispy flake hit her taste buds. Covering her lips so that she wouldn't drool in front of them, she added, "I guess we'll find out tomorrow."

"I don't really give a fuck where they put us," Keith shrugged with indifference as he looked pointedly over at the buffet counters. "Whatever our jobs are, no matter how shit they might be, at least we've got good food, soft beds and a hot shower. You can't argue with that."

"I could," Jesse glanced over his shoulder before lowering his voice. "Sure, people have got everything they need here.

184

But it's not gonna last forever. What happens when it all goes away? Or, even worse, what happens when people *realize* that it's all gonna go away? It'll be like us leaving Redhurst all over again, only this time, everybody in this room has already killed somebody to survive – and they won't hesitate to do it again."

Riley stopped chewing as she stared around the restaurant.

One lone woman was sobbing silent tears as she ate a bowl of rainbow-colored cereal.

Sitting on the floor in a corner, a little boy was eating chicken nuggets with his fingers, but in his other hand, he was white-knuckle clenching an unused fork.

At a nearby table, a grouch of a man had his entire body hunched over his breakfast. He glanced from side to side with every mouthful, one tense arm curled around his plate, as if he was unearthing a hidden treasure and swallowing the evidence.

All of these people had witnessed horrible things while they were out on the road, and whether they had been the victims or the perpetrators, they had been forced to shed their humanity in order to survive.

There was no denying the truth.

Every last one of them would kill out of self-preservation.

Even just for a meal.

Just like Riley had last night.

"What the fuck are you mumbling about?" Keith asked as he swallowed his mouthful, cocking an eyebrow at his son. "Drummond's got a plan to make this place self-sustaining. We put in the work they want us to do, and there'll be plenty to go around. We're probably not gonna be eating like this every day, but at least we're fucking eating. Think about it for a second – if they're feeding us like this, what makes you think that any of this shit's just gonna up and disappear?"

"Maybe you're right," Jesse began in that condescending tone of his that he had been brandishing lately. "Maybe the army's thinking that one day this'll all be over, and they wanna be remembered as heroes. Maybe they're helping people outta the goodness of their hearts. Or maybe it's more business than charity. Soldiers need supplies. Supplies need a workforce."

"I don't see how any of that makes a difference," Riley shrugged as she started on the slice of margarita pizza. "As long as we're getting fed, who gives a shit what their reasons are?"

"The reason why they're helping us doesn't really matter," he paused for a moment, studying them both, making sure that his words were sinking in. "What I'm saying is, what happens when they don't need us anymore, and they start kicking people out one by one? I was there for Drummond's speech last night. Fences, windmills, farms, all that good shit. But after everything's set up, do we really need this many people? I'll be fine – I'm a good little mechanic, apparently. But Joe Blow's gonna have a tough time trying to argue why he's worth keeping around."

"Can you believe this shit?" Keith scoffed, turning to Riley.

"Dad, I'm serious," Jesse kicked his chair back slightly, glancing pointedly down at his trouser pocket, where he had stashed a handful of plastic-wrapped hotel-branded biscuits. "This place isn't gonna last forever. We need a Plan B."

Hearing those words, Riley could see people already beginning to safeguard themselves.

Chelsea Preston was toying with her hair as she sat beside Wheeler, the burly blonde-bearded grunt unabashedly sizing her up over breakfast.

Calvin Fisher had already moved on to another group of newcomers, leaning down over their table with a sympathetic expression, his piercing blue gaze hiding a hint of eagerness.

"He's right," as much as Riley hated to admit it, Jesse had a point. "If people start thinking that they're at risk of getting kicked out, this place is gonna fall apart. Having a Plan B – just in case – isn't such a bad idea."

"Fuck this, I'm going up for round two," Keith decided, snatching up his empty plate and starting back towards the buffet counters. "Don't let me catch you two talking that shit to anybody else, because if you stir up these folks bad enough, it'll be a self-fulfilling prophecy. Understood?"

"Yeah, I guess," Riley exchanged a knowing glance with Jesse across the table.

"Riley?" he tested, his eyebrows raised.

"Fine, yes," she met Keith's stony gaze. "Just do me a favor – don't tell anyone where my mom went."

"Why the fuck would –"

"WHAT THE FUCK IS THIS SHIT!?" Halsey's nasal voice cut across the clatter and chatter of the restaurant.

Riley's head whipped around to see Chelsea flinching away from Wheeler, the blonde-bearded grunt's hand still gripping her thigh.

Swinging his half-empty bottle of bourbon, Halsey cracked the back of the soldier's skull, sending him to the floor as Chelsea screamed in horror.

The drunken ex-cultist stared down at his bottle – still intact – before keeling over and falling to his knees beside Wheeler.

Halsey raised the bottle again, bearing down on the back of the fallen soldier's neck, when Keith spear-tackled him from the side.

"Fuck off me!" Halsey yelled as everyone else in the restaurant clambered to their feet for a better view. "Chelsea, we're leaving. We're better off on our own. I'm not staying here if these fuckers are gonna pull this shit!!"

Riley and Jesse squeezed past the other survivors to see Sergeant Turnbull and a few other off-duty soldiers cutting through the crowd.

Wheeler was unconscious, coffee dribbling from his slack mouth into his blonde beard.

Keith had Halsey pinned face down, with one arm twisted behind his back.

"Trask, Rodriguez," Turnbull summoned the soldiers to her side. "Get these two outta here. I'll deal with them shortly. Everybody else, report to your assigned stations. You've all got work to do."

The crowd of onlookers began filing out of the restaurant, Chelsea leading the exodus without a backwards glance.

"Ungrateful rats," Trask growled as the heavy-handed brute marched towards the tangled trio of bodies.

"Keith had nothing to do with this," Rodriguez spoke up on his behalf as she stepped in front of the surly soldier.

"You two on a first-name basis now?" Trask cocked an eyebrow at her. He leaned in close, balefully dropping his tone, "We don't mix with them."

"Back off," the Latina soldier stared him down before looking back at Sergeant Turnbull. "This guy, Halsey – he's the one you want. He came in drunk outta his mind and assaulted Wheeler. Keith stopped him."

"Bullshit!" Halsey growled into the carpet, "That fucker was assaulting –"

"Shut your mouth or I'll pop your shoulder out," Keith

188

warned with a jerk of his arm.

"Take him away," Turnbull nodded at Trask before eyeing Keith. "Bowman, last night, you mentioned you were a police officer."

"Yeah, that's right," Keith answered, moving aside as Trask took over.

"I need somebody on crowd control," the oxlike officer stooped to lift Wheeler with her robust arms, draping his limp body over one thick shoulder. "Better that it comes from another civilian than from one of us. You start tomorrow."

Riley locked eyes with Jesse, both of them knowing that it wouldn't matter what they said to convince Keith that the hotel was a powder keg just waiting to explode – there was no way that he would listen to either of them now.

CHAPTER 34

"We've got a long ways to go," the ghost of Nolan Armstrong murmured in the driver's seat of their family's red suburban. "And I need him focused."

A knock at the door stirred Riley from the best sleep she'd had in months.

Stretching with a yawn, she tossed aside her sheets and planted her feet on the floor. Searching the darkness of the luxury hotel suite, her scarred fingers brushed against the lamp she'd unplugged.

Picking it up, she rose from the sofa and crept towards the door's peephole, squinting at Rodriguez standing on the other side.

Lowering the lamp, but not letting go, Riley opened the door, its security chain pulling tight as she blinked at the light streaming in from the corridor.

"Rise and – oh," Rodriguez frowned at the sight of her peering out through the gap. "I'm sorry, I thought this was Keith's room." She glanced over her shoulder at the other doors lining the corridor. "Do you know which one it is?"

"It's this one," Riley replied, her ears pricking up as Keith grunted his way out of bed.

"I'm an idiot," the Latina soldier's shoulders dropped slightly as she shook her head with a self-critical smile. "I didn't realize you two were together."

"Could you give us one second?" Riley shut the door in the woman's face, snickering to herself in the darkness.

"Who is it?" Keith's whiskey-cured voice croaked as he flicked the bathroom's light on.

"Your new girlfriend," she sassed him from the shadows with half a smirk. "What was that you said about me moving quick?"

"Fuck outta here," he chuckled over the sound of running water before he began brushing his teeth. "Just tell her I need a couple minutes."

Unlocking the security chain, Riley swung the door open wide, belatedly remembering that she was still holding a weapon, with Rodriguez's eyes snapping towards the lamp clutched in her hand.

"It's not what you think," Riley reassured her, looking up and down the empty corridor before setting the lamp down on the floor. She jerked her head towards the bathroom, "We aren't – I mean, we're not..."

Rodriguez raised her eyebrows patiently.

"Keith was my dad's partner," Riley explained, before her eyes widened with panic, and she quickly added, "I mean, on the force. The police force."

Just shut up already, she mentally kicked herself for almost accidentally cock-blocking the man. *Twice in one morning. May as well just slam the door in her face again.*

"We've been on the road together since the day the shit hit the fan," Keith stuck his head out of the bathroom, speaking around his toothbrush. "We lost Nolan early on. Ever since then, I've been watching over his daughter as if she was my own."

Riley cocked her head slightly at the claim, but she let him have his moment.

"So that's why you're all together," Rodriguez supposed, leaning in to see Jesse sleeping through the entire conversation in his bed beside the window.

"I insisted," Riley replied, glancing back at her sheets puddled at the foot of the sofa. "Just in case this place didn't turn out to be what we thought it was. I figured having the three of us sleeping in the same room was better than one and two."

"Smart move," Rodriguez admitted, before tilting her head with a smile, "But you're letting that perfectly good bed in your own room go to waste. Keith, I'll be waiting for you downstairs in the lobby. See you in five."

After spending most of yesterday enjoying everything that the hotel had to offer, Riley had decided that maybe the soldiers had the right idea after all. She was still wary of some of the other survivors though, who always seemed to be working an angle.

Calvin Fisher was just one example, but there were plenty of other people probing for information. Their curious questions had ranged from where she'd been and what she'd seen, her most useful scavenging techniques, the top five unlikely places where she'd found something worthwhile, along with any other communities that she might have come across in her travels, whether ravaged or still intact.

A few sweet-talking salesmen had already established an unofficial marketplace for anybody seeking a different job. If a person's skills matched the position's requirements and they had something of value to offer as a finder's fee, they'd be assigned a spot on a different crew. Although according to some of the more seasoned hotel guests, those who had traded jobs found that it was simply a case of the grass being greener on the other side.

Needless to say, Riley had quickly earned herself a reputation for staring the sycophantic survivors into submissive silence, and they learned to leave her alone.

Breakfast was a far more modest meal than yesterday's had been, with only two options to choose from – scrambled eggs on toast, or honey-flavored oatmeal.

There was a sobering stillness in the air as everyone quietly sat down to eat their food, grateful to have full stomachs, yet still wearing their familiar somber expressions as they remembered that their lives would never be the same again.

Riley was scraping up the dregs of her oatmeal when Captain Drummond entered the restaurant, the clatter of cutlery dying down as people looked up from their plates, pointing and whispering.

"Good morning, ladies and gentlemen," he addressed them all, his soldiers flanking him on either side. "You're probably wondering what happened to all the food! Relax, we still have more than plenty to go around. Every time we have a wave of new arrivals, we like to remind everyone what's possible around here. I am one hundred percent certain that with your hard work and commitment to helping build this community to be the best that it can be, we'll be able to eat like yesterday, every day. Like my daddy always said – *work like a slave, eat like a king*. So finish up, because it's time for you to earn that crown."

Drummond turned to the chef standing behind the counter,

ordering himself scrambled eggs on toast while everybody else dutifully downed their last few mouthfuls and murmured their farewells to each other.

"Good luck, wherever they're putting you," Jesse Bowman rose to his feet beside Riley as they joined the stream of survivors leaving the restaurant.

"Thanks," she rubbed the back of her neck, glad that she had remembered to wear her hair tie this time.

Corporal Newman was standing alone beside the exit, scanning the encouraged faces of each civilian preparing for the day's work.

"Hey, Armstrong," the short and stocky soldier picked her out of the crowd. "Somebody put your name on the shit-kicker shift. Come with me."

"Who the hell put me there?" Riley furrowed her eyebrows, matching his pace as they strode into the lobby and marched towards the front entrance.

Whatever the shit-kicker shift was, it didn't sound good.

"Your friend put you there," Newman spoke over his shoulder, trailing behind a dozen other workers being escorted out of the hotel, "After he put Wheeler into a fucking coma."

"You're not serious," Riley's jaw dropped open. She didn't realize how hard Halsey must have hit the man. "Hold on, that had nothing to do with me. Why am I getting punished?"

"You know how it is," Newman shrugged as they stepped outside into the frosty morning air. "Your friend. Our friend. A little reminder to make sure it never happens again."

"Well, that's bullshit," her breath misted in the pale winter sun. "If I knew I was gonna be freezing my ass off for what somebody else did, I would've picked up that bottle of bourbon and drank it down before finishing the job myself. I mean,

I might as well have some fun if I'm gonna get blamed for it anyway, right?"

"You just earned yourself another month of shit-kicking," Newman stopped in his tracks with a cold sidelong stare. "Have fun with that little outburst? Go ahead, say something else, I'll make sure you get stuck out here until the snow melts."

CHAPTER 35

Clamping her mouth shut, Riley Armstrong glared at Corporal Newman as she pulled the zipper of her charcoal gray thermal vest up to her neck.

Taking her seething silence as her submission, Newman led her down the chateau's snow-blanketed driveway and out to where the road was buried. Slogging through the slush, they turned right along the sidewalk, following a mess of freshly-churned footprints.

Riley was silently grateful for the weatherproof material lining her ski pants and hiking boots. If she had still been wearing her old jeans and sneakers, her feet would have been iced over within a matter of minutes.

Skirting around the construction fence, they circled back into the adjacent empty lot at the foot of the chateau. On the other side of the yard, Riley saw the dozen other workers of the shit-kicker shift already huddled together, gathered around a bunch of snow shovels with dour expressions.

"Alright, listen up!" Newman shouted across the sprawling lot. "As you can see, we had a snowstorm last night, and it's fucked up all of our hard work over the past week. First thing we need to do is clear a path from the hotel's loading bay out to the bridge. Then when we hit the road, we're gonna need enough room for a bus to fit through. I know – it's a raw deal, but it's the best deal you're gonna get. Now, you can bitch. You can moan. You can cry icicles for all I care. I don't really give a fuck what you do, as long as you get it done."

Long plumes of breath escaped from every laborer's mouth, each one of them letting out a heavy sigh before picking up a shovel and getting to work.

"Heather?" Riley called as she caught sight of the fiery redhead cursing under her breath. She glanced at the bandage wrapped around the girl's wrist, "I thought for sure you'd be outta action for a while."

"Yeah, you really fucked this hand up," Heather's husky voice came back as she struggled to dig with one arm, cradling her shovel in the crook of her elbow and against her hip. "That was the doctor's official diagnosis, word for word. He said four weeks rest, a box of ibuprofen, and a follow-up appointment before he'd even *think* about clearing me for work."

"So, what the hell are you doing out here?" Riley frowned as she tossed aside a scoop of snow.

"That Piss Beard Wheeler slipped into a fucking coma," Heather grimaced as she strained to find a rhythm that worked. The snow shovel dropped from her arm, and a shadow crossed her face, "I swear, the next time I see Halsey, I'm gonna break his damn nose again with this motherfucking piece of shit bitch shovel!"

"That's the spirit, ladies!" Newman yelled as he and his grunts kept watch over the line of laborers. "Get angry. Get furious! Use all that extra energy to get that path dug! The sooner we're done out here, the sooner we're all inside again."

"You want this shit done faster?" Riley paused as she glanced back at the corporal. "Grab a shovel and give us a hand."

The other workers chuckled at the suggestion, already knowing the chances.

"And who's gonna watch your back if we get hit by raiders?" Newman asked rhetorically, before he and his soldiers started towards the former construction lot's site office. "That reminds me. We should probably go sit down and have a coffee. It'll help to keep us alert. You're welcome."

"Asshole," Riley glowered at him before tossing aside another scoop.

"Told you," said a voice on her left. It belonged to the same sunken-eyed wafer-thin woman from yesterday in the restaurant. "Only the soldiers can sit around all day long doing nothing."

"You don't say?" Heather turned her fuming frustration into mocking sarcasm, "Thank you for your little gem of wisdom, whoever you are. I'll be sure to make a note of it in my journal tonight so I don't forget."

"Esmee Gallagher," the haggard woman brushed off the barb, her gaze lingering on the two girls.

"Riley," she replied, jerking her head, "This is Heather."

"I saw Calvin sitting with you yesterday," Esmee began as she stooped to lift her shovel, "Did you tell him anything?"

Here we go, Riley thought to herself. *Another creep fishing for information.*

Grunting in annoyance, she turned back to shoveling snow.

With the stretch of silence lengthening down the line of laborers, Riley felt as though her time on the shit-kicker shift was going to last forever.

"This place changed him," Esmee let the question go unanswered. "It changes everyone, eventually. The people you see here are those of us who still have a conscience."

"Did you know Calvin before you came here?" Riley narrowed her eyes at the woman.

"I like to think that I did," she smiled sadly. "But now, I'm not so sure... I was with him on the night his parents got murdered. A gang of bikers showed up while we were having dinner on the side of the freeway, and everybody started shooting. He would've died there too, if it wasn't for me."

"You were the nurse," Riley realized, remembering Calvin's story back at the golf course in Kansas. "How long have you guys been here?"

"Not as long as him," Esmee replied with a pained wince as she tossed a scoop of snow. "After he got back on his feet, he went out on a supply run and just disappeared on us. We looked for him, but after weeks went by without a trace, we just figured that he didn't wanna be found. I thought that maybe being around us reminded him of the night that he lost his parents. Then one day, he showed up again with a bunch of soldiers, and they told us all to get on the buses. Nobody trusted it. We lost so many good people that day – all so that Calvin could meet his fucking recruitment quota for the month."

"Recruitment quota?" Riley echoed in confusion, furrowing her eyebrows.

"First, they give you everything," Esmee looked along the line of laborers, those within earshot nodding in agreement. "Then, little by little, they start taking it all back. If your work's not up to the soldiers' standards, your room gets smaller, your shower gets colder, and you get put on rations. At the end of the month, they assess your performance, and your status changes accordingly."

Riley didn't want to believe it, and yet somehow, it all made sense.

Calvin hadn't cared about her mother's pregnancy, or about reuniting their group.

He just needed to get his fucking numbers up.

"Looks like civilization isn't dead after all," Heather supposed with a cynical smile. "First rule of society – exploit whoever you can, and reward anyone stupid enough to play the game with a bunch of shiny shit that they'll never be able to keep."

"Slaves to comfort," Riley agreed bitterly, staring up at the chateau with resentment. She turned back to Esmee, "Hold on, if you're a nurse, why are you out here shoveling snow? Shouldn't you be in the hotel with all the other medical staff?"

"I refused to treat the soldiers who shot my friends," Esmee answered with another pained wince, glancing over her shoulder at the group of grunts idly watching from the site office. "They thought it would be funny to watch me work for them in other ways."

"What happens if you don't work at all?" Heather asked, sizing up the length of the trench that they had dug so far. They still had a long way to go. "I'm sick of this shit already."

"Dead weight's better off dead," one eavesdropping worker remarked beside Heather.

"They're killing the people who don't work?" Riley glanced down the line of laborers. "That's fucking slavery."

"It's just a rumor," Esmee shook her head, dispelling the claim. "Anybody who stops pulling their weight gets kicked out, and we never see them again. I like to think they're doing well on their own though."

"Kinda wish we went with Ralph, back when we had the chance," another laborer lamented as he dug. "Now winter's here and that ship's sailed."

"Some of our friends decided they didn't wanna live like this," Esmee explained, turning back to Riley and Heather. "They'd had enough of climbing the cut-throat ladder here, and they just decided to break away and figure things out for themselves. Ralph said he knew a place not too far from here."

"Ah, Ralph," the man working beside Heather clucked his tongue and stared up at the pale winter sun. *"Never trust somebody who doesn't eat red meat.* You got that one wrong, Pa."

"This Ralph guy," Riley swallowed the lump building in her throat as she glanced sidelong at Heather. "He didn't happen to be a pescatarian, did he?"

"That's a hell of a guess," Esmee gazed back at her.

CHAPTER 36

"Fuck, fuck, fuck, fuck, fuck," Riley Armstrong murmured as soon as the elevator doors shut behind them. The walls shook as she stomped the handrail with her snow-caked hiking boot, "FUCK!!"

"I'm getting outta here," Heather decided, her breathing becoming shallow as she began to hyperventilate in the small space. "Tonight. Fuck it. You're coming – you're coming with me, right?"

Riley stared up at the flashing floor numbers as the elevator climbed the building.

It was the first thing she wanted to do.

It was the last thing they could afford to do.

"We've gotta keep our cool," she forced herself to speak in a measured tone, despite the outrage threatening to consume her.

"I've kept it – I kept it all fucking day," Heather fumed between gasps for air, doubling over at the waist with her good hand clutching her thigh. "We *murdered* those peop–"

She retched the rest of her sentence, vomiting into the corner.

The elevator's bell chimed, and Riley hauled the reeling redhead out into the corridor.

"Listen," she whispered into Heather's ear as they made their way back towards their rooms. "We have to do this quietly, or we're dead. If this gets out – fucking hell – if the soldiers don't kill us first, the other survivors will."

Riley doubted that anyone would support their claim of being manipulated by Turnbull and her grunts into massacring dozens of innocent civilians.

The more likely scenario was that the other hotel guests would simply keep their mouths shut – more worried about their monthly performance assessments – rather than listen to the inconvenient truth about the people who were keeping them all fed.

And there was no way that Riley was going to risk telling Esmee and the rest of the shit-kicker shift that she'd played a part in slaughtering all of their friends.

"Shit," Heather breathed, wiping her mouth as she stared down the corridor.

There was a housekeeping cart parked outside her room, one of the housemaids standing in the doorway, swapping out her bed sheets.

"Come on, we can talk this out in my room," Riley stopped beside her door, pulling out her key card to swipe the lock.

The door's light flashed red.

She gave it a moment before trying again.

The door's light flashed red.

"What the fuck?" Riley frowned before crossing the corridor to Heather's room. She leaned over the cleaning cart, "Excuse me? My key card's not working."

"You'll have to speak to reception," the housemaid replied

from around the corner.

The two girls exchanged an edgy glance.

"Hey, it's cool, you don't have to change the sheets," Heather pushed the cart aside with her hip, before edging through the doorway into her room. "I'm happy with the way it was."

"Get back!" the housemaid stepped out from behind the wall, holding a walkie up to her lips. "Don't make me call security. This room's been reassigned. Please, just leave me alone so I can do my job."

"We're going, we're going!" Riley reached in and yanked Heather back out into the corridor. "We'll talk to reception. It's probably just a mistake. No need to call anyone."

"Fuck, this is going from bad to worse," Heather hissed as they strode back towards the elevator hall. "I'm so fucking stupid. This is Taylor-level dumb."

"Relax, alright?" Riley kept her breathing steady as she mashed the button. "Let's just get back downstairs before that lady calls the soldiers on us."

"No, you don't understand," Heather snarled as she paced back and forth. "I hid my knife after the raid. I had it on me all day yesterday. And then this morning, I thought we were safe, so I stashed it in my fucking mattress."

The bell chimed as Riley stared back at her.

"Yep, that was pretty fucking dumb," she nodded in agreement before stepping inside the elevator. "Come on. Try not to hurl inside this one."

"Bitch," Heather exhaled as they rode down to the lobby. "If they're already onto us, what makes you think that we're gonna be any better off downstairs?"

"Nobody's onto us," Riley replied, hoping that it was true. "Nobody knows anything about the raid except for us and the

204

soldiers. And all they've done is made us shovel snow."

"So, we're just supposed to pretend that everything's normal?" Heather shot back. "How the fuck are you so cool about all this?"

Riley flexed her gloved fingers, glowering at the elevator doors as they opened.

"I'm not," she answered with ice in her tone, keeping her gaze locked on the lobby so that she wouldn't stab Heather with the daggers in her eyes.

Survivors and soldiers alike crisscrossed the hotel's lobby, some doggedly returning from their shifts, others on their way to hit the gym, or heading towards the restaurant for dinner.

The two women's boots drummed across the hardwood floor as they approached the front desk.

"Good evening, ladies," the receptionist greeted them warmly, "How may I assist you?"

"My door's not opening," Riley placed her key card on the desk.

"And my room's been reassigned, apparently," Heather tossed hers on the counter as well.

"Ah, yes, I did receive a note earlier today," the clerk scanned their cards and peered at his computer screen. "Just as I thought. Congratulations Miss Armstrong, Miss Seabrook, you're officially roommates. You might notice that the standard suites are a little bit cozier than your previous accommodations, but at least the elevator ride's not as long. Let me just recode your cards to your new room."

"Fucking Halsey," Heather muttered under her breath.

"I had some clothes in my old room," Riley realized that she hadn't washed her gray hoodie and jeans last night. "Have they been moved to the new one?"

"You'll find that your closet has been adequately stocked with winter-wear," he smiled as he handed them back their cards. "Anything that isn't appropriate for the snow will have been bagged, tagged, and sent off to storage until spring. We wouldn't want anybody getting sick!"

"That reminds me," Heather held up her bandaged wrist, "I had a box of ibuprofen on my nightstand."

"I see," the receptionist tightened his lips in an annoyingly courteous manner. "Unfortunately, your room's status isn't cleared for medicinal privileges – hence why we don't want anybody getting sick."

"What the fuck?" she blustered, leaning over the counter. "How the hell do you expect me to work with a busted wrist and no meds?"

"Yes, I can certainly understand your frustration," he recited a well-rehearsed line, before offering a sheepish shrug. "And while we appreciate you highlighting your concerns, our hands are tied in this matter. Army directives outrank both the doctor's orders and our hotel's policies. But you're more than welcome to appeal the decision with a military officer. Would you like for me to arrange an appointment?"

"That won't be necessary," Riley nudged Heather as she reached for her key card. "Thank you."

"Easy for you to say," the fiery redhead scowled sidelong at her as they made their way towards the restaurant. "Don't think I've forgotten who fucked up my wrist in the first place."

They joined the line of survivors queuing up for the two dinner options – fried trout on a bed of jasmine rice, or a steaming serve of chicken and mushroom risotto.

Riley spotted Chelsea Preston up ahead, the blonde vegan asking the chefs if they could remove the juicy chunks of

206

chicken from her risotto.

"Hey, Chelsea," she leaned sideways out of the line, waiting for the former college girl to make eye contact. "Have you seen Halsey around?"

"Who?" Chelsea frowned back, shaking her head without a hint of recognition before snatching her plate off the counter, resolving to set aside the meat herself.

"Wow, and I've been calling you a bitch this whole time," Heather chuckled aloud as they watched the pregnant blonde girl approach a table full of soldiers.

"Guess she's shopping around for an upgrade," Riley gave her a small snort as they collected their fried fish. "Keep an eye out for Keith and Halsey. They need to know the truth about the raid."

Searching the restaurant, she spotted Jesse Bowman sitting alone by the window, and they crossed the room towards his table.

"Hey, how'd you guys go today?" he covered his mouth as they sat down, still oblivious to the soldiers' horrendous deception.

"You were right about Calvin," Riley said to his delight, filling him in on what Esmee had told them, while Heather kept her eyes peeled for Keith and Halsey.

"I'm not gonna lie," Jesse sat back in his chair with a victorious grin on his face, "I don't hate saying this at all – I fucking told you we couldn't trust him. I told you that night at the golf course. *I don't trust this guy. Let me search his bag for a walkie.* And look what happened. Hold on, I think I sense an apology coming my way."

"Are you done?" Riley raised her eyebrows patiently.

"Fine, I'm happy with you admitting that I was right," he

gloated before finally settling down again. "But are you sure you've thought his offer through? I mean, as much as I don't like Calvin, I was thinking about what he said – Susan and Abbie *would* be better off here, especially with all the doctors and midwives on hand. And if anything happened to this place, at least we'd all be back together again."

Riley drew back, cocking her head slightly.

Something had changed about him since yesterday.

For the first time in a long time, Jesse Bowman was optimistic about their situation.

She wondered whether he would have made the same suggestion if he knew the details about the raid, but she didn't want to burden him with the weight of it just yet.

His picture of positivity was a welcome change from the norm.

"Okay, let's look past the reason why we all split up in the first place," she began, having spent most of last night mulling over Calvin's offer on the sofa. "Do you really think that Virge and Sterling would trust a bunch of armed strangers after what happened with Shepherd? No. There's a strong chance that whoever gets on that bus to pick them up won't be coming back. Either that, or we'll end up getting one of our friends killed."

"But Virge was ex-military," Jesse reasoned, pointedly glancing at the soldiers in the restaurant. "Maybe he'll listen to them long enough not to shoot."

"Did you hear the way he talked about the army?" she furrowed her eyebrows at him, as if they hadn't shared the same campfires for three months straight. "He gave them his legs, and they tossed him out like he was nothing but used goods."

"Shit," Heather spoke over her shoulder as she watched the entrance, "If that was me, I'd start shooting based on that alone."

"Alright," Jesse conceded, before lowering his voice. "Well, we should probably move somewhere quieter if we're gonna work on our Plan B."

"No, Plan B's out," Riley replied, flexing her gloved fingers underneath the table before leaning towards him. "We need to work on getting the fuck outta here."

"I think we might have a problem," Heather stared pointedly at the front of the restaurant.

Marching through the entrance alongside Rodriguez, Corporal Newman, and a slew of other soldiers fresh from the gym, Keith Bowman was practically an honorary member of the military movement in Colorado.

CHAPTER 37

Riley Armstrong waved the former police officer over to their table by the window.

Keith Bowman excused himself from the group of grunts crowding the counters, asserting that he'd rather have dinner with his son than smell the soldiers' sweat-stained uniforms while he was trying to eat.

"Thanks for the save," he grinned as he sat down with a steaming serve of chicken and mushroom risotto. "I gotta say – this job is the tits. It doesn't even feel like I've worked today. Nobody wants to piss off the soldiers. All I've done is lift, eat, hit the bar, hit the rec room, and do it all over again."

Heather chuckled with a sidelong glance at Riley, knowing that they were just about to burst his bubble.

"We can't stay here," Riley said flatly, watching his grin fade.

"What the fuck?" he frowned at her incredulously. "Not this shit again, Riley. This is the best we've had it in months, and you know it. Fuck me – this is better than I had it back in Redhurst. Three square meals a day that aren't burning on the outside and still frozen in the middle. A bed that doesn't fuck my back harder than I can at the gym. Shit, I don't even have to change the sheets anymore. Halsey said it best – this is a damn vacation. Why would you ever wanna leave?"

"You're probably the only person who's enjoying this place, Dad," Jesse explained, gesturing at the other exhausted survivors around the restaurant. "Everybody else is practically slave labor around here. This isn't as good as it seems on the surface. We need to start planning for what happens when people start to realize that maybe they're better off on their own."

"I thought you of all people would've been happy here," Keith turned his stony gaze on his son. "You get to work on cars all day long. You used to do that for free, so don't give me this *slave labor* bullshit. Or is this that Palmview privilege talking now – you think you're too good for punching the clock for a living?"

"It's not that," Riley interjected, trying to save the man from making an even bigger ass out of himself. "Keith, the soldiers lied to us."

"About what?" he scoffed, not even giving her enough time to answer, "Whatever it is, it doesn't make a difference. Because I'll tell you what I know. Last week, we were splitting a packet of chips five ways for our one daily meal. You remember that? I sure fucking do. I woke up one night trying to eat a hole through my sleeping bag. That's how damn hungry I was. But yesterday, we ate like fucking royalty. Drummond's got this place under control. As long as we stay here, and we do what they want us to do, we'll never have to starve again."

"Those people at the school weren't cannibals," Heather cut through the noise of the conversation, getting straight to the point.

Keith sucked his front teeth and stared up at the ceiling, shaking his head in silence.

"If you don't believe us," Riley looked pointedly towards Esmee, the former nurse sitting at a table near the bathroom, "Go ask that woman about a man named Ralph. Fucking pescatarian. Wore a pair of glasses. And only a few months ago, led a whole group of survivors to Leadthorne High, because they didn't wanna be slaves to a bunch of deserters."

"*A few months*, Riley," Keith picked the one part of her argument that supported his perspective. "That's long enough for anybody to get desperate enough." He was still deep in denial, refusing to consider the consequences of any other possibility. Picking up his plate, he stood, eyeing the two girls, "If you wanna leave, that's up to you. But you're not dragging me – or my boy – anywhere with you."

"Fine, stay here with your new friends," Riley scowled up at him as he turned his back on them. "Just remember, only a couple days ago, those same soldiers were kicking the shit outta you. I hope your jaw still hurts every time you eat like fucking royalty."

She watched Keith rejoin the soldiers at their table, slumping down into an empty chair.

"I dunno what happened at that school," Jesse tore Riley's spiteful gaze away from Keith, "But if what you're saying is true – if those people were innocent – he's gonna fall apart. And nobody else around here is gonna take care of him but me."

Jesse blinked down at his plate in sudden realization, and he sat back in his chair, shaking his head with a smile.

"What's so funny?" Riley cocked an eyebrow at him.

"Oh, nothing," his gaze went from the table back up to his

212

father across the room. "It's just – all this time, I thought he was holding me back, trying to keep me safe from what the world's become. Now, I'm realizing I never even needed his permission in the first place. I've been holding myself back just for his sake, so that he doesn't have to worry about me. But this time, it's different. If I leave, I'm gonna be the one worrying about him. I'm sorry, Riley. I'm not going anywhere."

"That's so thoughtful of you," Heather mocked him with her husky voice, before turning to Riley. "Speaking for myself though – I'm not spending one more day shoveling snow for these sadistic sons of bitches who just mind-fucked us into murdering a bunch of civilians."

Riley nodded, turning her gaze between the two as she weighed up her options.

She didn't want to work for these manipulative monsters any more than Heather.

If she decided to leave, then winter was the perfect opportunity. The falling snow could cover their tracks while simultaneously making it impossible for the tour buses to follow them. They couldn't afford to wait for warmer weather – once the snow was gone, it would be too late.

If she chose to stay though, she would have access to food, water and shelter, for as long as she continued to cooperate. After a few monthly assessments, she could work her way back up the ranks, and eventually even switch over to a job that she might actually enjoy.

But surrendering to those comforts would mean looking past the blood on her hands.

CHAPTER 38

"Riley, wait up!" Calvin Fisher called as he caught up to her in the lobby.

The laborers of the shit-kicker shift were on their way out for another grueling day of shoveling snow. Heather and Esmee gave Riley one backwards glance before trudging outside into the pale winter morning.

"What do you want from me, Calvin?" Riley snapped, turning back to face him.

"Uh, nothing," he was caught off guard by the sudden edge in her voice. "I just wanted to help you get your mom and the rest of –"

"Bullshit," she cut him off, before he could dig himself any deeper into his pit of lies. "All you care about is your fucking recruitment quota. Esmee already told me the whole story."

"She did, did she?" Calvin ran a thumb along his jaw line, eyeing the back of the former nurse as she and the others descended into the snow. "Do you really trust her over me?"

"At this point, I'd trust anyone over you," Riley shot back, her doubts about him deepening every time he opened his mouth.

"Don't be like that," his piercing blue gaze attempted to

soften for her sympathy, only needling at her even harder.

The stubborn jut of her chin broke his confident demeanor, and his mask fell.

"Please, Riley," Calvin begged, his boyish charm disappearing into desperation. "I just need one more person to round out this month. I'm so close. They said that if I can deliver, they'll let me keep my suite until spring. You can take the bed if you want. I don't care. I'll take the sofa. Just tell me where your mom is and I'll take care of the rest."

Riley supposed that if they were sharing the same room, she could just coast on his accomplishments, instead of having to work her way back up the ranks.

She didn't even have to think about it.

"Alright, fine," she sighed in feigned submission. "It's a little bit hazy, but from what I remember, all you need to do is take the interstate south through New Mexico. Drive east after you cross over the border into Texas, maybe a couple of hours, and then when the freeway splits, you take the north route for about forty miles to go fuck yourself. You piece of shit. Fuck you, you selfish son of a bitch. I'm not telling you a damn thing."

"I really hoped you'd be the one to help me out," Calvin's tone hardened again with a flash of his roguish grin. "You're not the only lead I'm chasing up on though. I remember you mentioned Heather had a sister, right? I wonder if she'd be willing to get Taylor back in exchange for a decent bed."

"Why don't you come on out and ask her?" Riley called him on his bluff, knowing that Heather would never give up her sister.

She held the hotel's front entrance open, inviting him outside, waiting for him to leave the warmth and comfort of the hotel's lobby.

His smile faded as he declined, instead turning towards another family of newcomers heading towards the elevators.

"Yeah, walk away, you fucking creep," Riley narrowed her eyes at the back of Calvin's head as a soldier approached to move her along. Casting caution to the wind, she yelled across the length of the lobby, "Don't tell that asshole anything! He's just trying to use you for a fucking room upgrade!!"

The family flashed a thumbs-up at her before quickly stepping inside an elevator.

With a bitter smile, Riley ventured out into the cold.

She didn't even bother to glance back to watch his reaction.

The Calvin that she had known was gone – this place had changed him.

And if she stayed here long enough, eventually she'd be at risk of betraying the people who trusted her just as easily.

CHAPTER 39

"Change of plans, everyone!" Corporal Newman shouted across the former construction site. "The snow came down on us hard again last night, so there's no point in clearing the road now. Buses aren't gonna make it out to where we're going anyway. So we're gonna use the snowmobiles to do this last scavenging run instead."

The huddled group of laborers grumbled among themselves, complaining that all of their snow-shoveling efforts yesterday had been for nothing.

"Fuck," Riley Armstrong muttered under her breath, glancing sidelong at Heather.

Their plan – their entire plan – had hinged on slipping into the thicket of evergreens lining the other side of the S-bend to make their escape. But if they weren't clearing the road anymore, they'd have a tough time of reaching the trees unnoticed.

"Don't go thinking you're about to get a day off though," Newman continued, nodding towards the delivery laneway that separated the hotel from the construction site. "Half of you are gonna stay here and clear the way to the loading bay.

The other half are going over to the garage so we can dig out the snowmobiles. Whoever finishes up first gets a hot shower tonight."

"Maybe we can give them the slip on the way to the garage," Heather murmured in Riley's ear. "Wherever they're keeping the vehicles, they've gotta use the road that runs past here to get to the bridge."

Foolish enough to think that they had any choice in the matter, the two women stepped forward to volunteer, only to watch as Newman began picking out workers at random, sending seven of them on their way to the garage with a pair of his grunts.

Exhaling a long plume of mist, Riley trudged through the snow towards the delivery laneway, lining up alongside Heather, Esmee, and three other survivors.

The wide laneway was bordered on three sides – the wall of the hotel, the construction fencing, and the roller door to the loading bay. At the far end of the delivery lane was the street access, where a separate group of guards were posted – as a safety precaution against any raiders with a mad ambition to hit the hotel's warehouse.

Riley and the other laborers settled into the steady routine of dig, scoop, toss, repeat.

Corporal Newman and his other soldier leaned up against the wall of the hotel, watching with boredom as puffs of snow flew over the construction fence. Waving at the group of guards down the lane, the duo soon moved towards the site office for their morning coffee.

"We need to rethink this plan," Riley whispered in between shovel tosses. "We're not getting outta here today."

"One thing changes, and you're just gonna give up?" Heather

cocked an eyebrow at her. "There's only two of them right now. We can take them."

"Two, plus anyone in shouting distance," Riley shook her head. "No, it's too risky. Even if nobody else was around, they're still soldiers. They're trained to kill. We're just a couple of amateurs compared to them. Like I said last night – if we can't sneak around the guards, then we're as good as dead."

"Fuck, Riley," Heather seethed as her shovel fell from her awkward one-handed grip. "This doesn't have to be that hard. We can do it just like back at the school. Pick a direction. Start running. Figure out all the other shit later."

"What'd you say about a school?" Esmee sidled closer, the sunken-eyed woman gazing at the two girls.

Riley's heart skipped a beat.

The other workers were staring sidelong at them too.

"Oh, we went to high school together," Heather replied casually. She chuckled at them with half a smirk, "You know, back when algebra was supposed to be some important life skill."

"No, you said *the* school," Esmee narrowed her eyes suspiciously.

"I don't care what she said," one of the laborers pushed past the former nurse. He stomped through the snow towards Heather, "We're already one man down, so pick up your fucking shovel and start digging. I haven't had a hot shower in weeks, and I'll be damned if I'm gonna let either of you two fuck this up for me."

"Hey, back off, dickhead," Riley warned, subtly turning her shovel's blade towards his kneecap.

His hand shot out faster than she had anticipated.

Riley tried to take a step back for distance, but her boot

dragged in the snow.

Wobbling in place, she caught his shove square in the chest, and he sent her stumbling backwards into the construction fence.

The chain-linked mesh jingled and warped as she shot back to her feet, hate in her eyes.

"You're right, I said *the* school," Heather stepped in between them, glancing back over her shoulder with a wink at Riley. "The soldiers told us there was a bunch of cannibals living in Leadthorne High. Sergeant Turnbull and Corporal Newman said if we eliminated the threat, we could stay here. And that's exactly what we did. We didn't realize who they were until yesterday, but all your friends are dead. Mike. Bree. Charlee. Ralph. We killed them."

"*You what!?*" Esmee exclaimed, tugging at her own hair in despair.

"What the fuck, Heather?" Riley breathed, her eyes going wide as she watched the laborers' faces working through shock, dismay, anguish and vengeance.

She turned to run towards the group of guards posted at the end of the laneway, when Heather seized her by the arm.

"Follow me," she pulled Riley towards the loading bay's closed roller door before the others could find their feet.

Slogging through the snow, Heather veered off to the side of the hotel's warehouse, thrusting her elbow in between the wall and the chain-linked fence, bending and stretching the mesh to squeeze in through the narrow gap.

Riley glanced back as a shout of alarm went up from the soldiers.

"YOU MOTHERFUCKERS!!" one of the laborers bellowed, brandishing his shovel and turning on the guards.

"How could you?" Esmee sank to her knees in heaving sobs, bawling in barren grief.

"I'm sorry, we didn't know," she choked before turning to follow Heather.

Riley forced herself along the side of the construction fence, but contending with the knee-deep snow and the cold embrace of the steel mesh, she found it impossible to drag her shovel along with her. She hated the idea of leaving without a weapon, but there was no other choice.

The chain-linked fence shook, squashed and strangled with every grating inch forward, but she kept her eyes on the back of Heather. After all, if the one-handed girl could squeeze her way through, Riley had no excuse.

Behind them in the laneway, the workers clashed with the soldiers, their shouts of rage and pain flying on the frigid winter wind.

Just as Riley thought that the tight crevice along the hotel's warehouse was going to stretch on forever, she burst free from the construction fence, collapsing into the snow on the other side.

"Let's go, let's go, let's go!" Heather urged through gritted teeth as she wrenched her back upright.

Riley glanced around to get her bearings.

To their left was the military blockade on the bridge, with sentries pointing and yelling, and one guard thumbing his walkie.

To their right was the hotel's courtyard and swimming pool, with doors slamming and combat boots drumming just around the corner.

The construction fence shook at their rear, and Riley drove her legs through the snow, sloshing straight towards the river of ice blocking their path.

CHAPTER 40

"Riley, we need to move," the ghost of Nolan Armstrong urged his shivering daughter forward, the heel of his hand pressing firmly between her shoulder blades.

"W–w–where are we?" Riley's teeth chattered uncontrollably as she gasped for air, every lungful of frost scalding her throat. She glanced around, dazed and confused. "Dad?"

Just a moment ago, they had been standing together in the sweltering parking lot of a Californian supermarket, empty-handed after losing their carts of water.

They certainly didn't need the water anymore, but she was a long way from home.

"Move your fucking legs, bitch!" a red-haired woman's husky voice roared from the snowy bank on the far side of the river.

"It's so c–c–cold," Riley complained, trembling in the water, despite her weatherproof ski pants and hiking boots.

Her clothing's level of winter resistance didn't make much of a difference, not when it came to standing waist-deep in a river of ice.

"Get a hold of yourself," another woman's voice growled

from behind.

SMACK!

A wet slap to the side of Riley's face knocked some sense back into her.

"Hurry up!" Esmee yelled in her ear, the former nurse tear-streaked yet determined, shoving her towards Heather waiting on the other side. "The only way we're gonna live through this is if we stay together."

She must have followed us, Riley thought to herself, letting Esmee guide her as she willed her numb feet through the swirling ice.

"Come on, I got you," Heather reached down with her good arm, clasping hold of Riley's gloved hand and wrenching her out of the river.

"That was so fucking stupid," Riley scolded herself, still shaking as they both bent to help Esmee up onto the snowy bank. "If that w–w–water was any deeper, we'd all be dead."

"Taylor-level dumb," Heather agreed, before nodding towards the first few soldiers stopping short of the river. "Looks like you bought us some time though."

"And we need to make every second count," Esmee huffed as she climbed the bank, clutching at the bony branches of the trees lining the riverside. "If we don't get dry soon, we're dead anyway."

Riley and Heather followed the former nurse up to where the highway was buried, turning away from the military blockade on the bridge.

They were knee-deep in the snow, making it almost impossible to walk, the three women having to wade through the white instead.

"Where the hell do you think you're going!?" Sergeant

Turnbull shouted from the other side of the river, the oxlike officer unmistakable between the bare-branched trees as she glowered at them.

"We'll be seeing you again, real soon," Trask promised, the surly soldier fighting the temptation to jump into the icy river after them. "Probably when the three of you rats realize there's no cheese to chew on out there."

Riley locked eyes with the boorish brute before flipping him the bird.

"Makes you wonder whether they have any ammo left," Heather panted red-faced, hugging her arms to her chest. "You'd think they would've opened fire by now."

"Maybe that's why they sent us to the school," Riley supposed, her breathing shallow between her shuddering teeth. She was getting worse by the minute. "They c–c–couldn't risk doing it themselves. But they need those bullets we left behind."

"That's what the scavenging mission's for," Heather realized, her striking green eyes gazing down the highway. "How far out do you think that school is?"

"Don't kid yourselves," Esmee spoke over her shoulder as she slogged through the snow. "They've got plenty of bullets. They just can't shoot at us right now because they have to keep up the charade. If anybody in the hotel sees the soldiers gunning us down for leaving, the whole place is gonna fall apart."

Riley gazed across the riverbank at the soldiers gathered around Turnbull.

The butch sergeant was quietly giving out orders to the armed men and women, each of them breaking off in pairs to usher any civilian onlookers back inside.

Sentries manning the blockade on the bridge were holding

their position, but they were tracking the three women with binoculars, with one occasionally murmuring into his walkie.

"Those g–g–guns at the school are gonna be our best shot at surviving," Riley replied, even though every step through the snow was becoming a battle.

"No, getting dry – is – our best," Esmee's speech began to slur as she swayed on the spot, her feet frozen. "Hypo – hypotherm…"

The wafer-thin woman wavered for a few more moments before falling face first into the snow.

"Shit!" Riley drove her legs towards her, puffing as she grabbed hold of Esmee's arm and pulled her up. She glanced back over her shoulder, "Help me carry her."

"What about the g–g–guns?" Heather mocked Riley's shivering stutter, before realizing that her own teeth were beginning to chatter now too.

"She's right – we're all gonna catch hypothermia," Riley grunted and grimaced, heaving the fallen woman towards a nearby cluster of apartments overlooking the river. "Whatever's happening to her now is gonna happen to us soon. She's the only one who c–c–can tell us what to do."

"But what *can* we do?" Heather asked, grabbing Esmee's other arm anyway. She glanced up at the rustic beige brick apartments, "This place would've been picked clean months ago. The soldiers could be on us any minute now, and we'll be trapped inside there with nothing to use."

"Better that than being c–c–caught face down in the snow out here," Riley countered, summoning her resolve as she sized up the nearest building.

The front door was missing, with a snowdrift piled high against its entrance, offering only a narrow opening at the top of the door frame.

"We're gonna have to crawl through," she turned to Heather, her brow creasing in a moment of clarity. "And so will the soldiers."

CHAPTER 41

Together, the two women hauled Esmee Gallagher through the apartment building's hallway and upstairs to the second level. All the while, the former nurse was slipping in and out of consciousness, slurring survival tips before her eyes glassed over again.

"Esmee, we don't have any tea or soup," Riley tried to remind the wafer-thin woman, but her voice fell on deaf ears.

"Forget it – grab some more curtains," Heather said as her fumbling fingers struggled to pull off Esmee's socks.

Their shivers and shakes had already subsided into jittery spells, but both of them were too exhausted from all the exertion to notice.

A rash of gooseflesh budded up Riley's legs as she lumbered across the damp corridor, stumbling barefoot into the next apartment to tear the curtains from the window.

Chancing a glance through the frosty glass at the hotel across the river, Riley could only see a mess of freshly-churned footprints littering the snowy bank on the far side.

There was no sign of the soldiers anymore.

She clumsily shuffled back to their apartment overlooking

the snow-buried highway, kneeling down to wipe Esmee's legs and feet dry.

"How long do you think we have?" Heather breathed hard as she turned their pants inside out, smearing icy crystals across the carpet.

"Can't say for sure," Riley admitted, draping the curtain over Esmee's torso, making sure to keep the woman's arms and legs uncovered, as instructed.

She crossed the room to the window.

A flurry of frosty flakes blew past as more snow began to fall over the empty highway.

"There's no way we'll be able to cover up our tracks," Riley continued, biting her bottom lip at the sight of their trail. "Not ones that deep. We'll either have to stay here long enough to heat up again before we make a run for those guns at the school, or we'll make our stand downstairs when they come in through the door."

"Either one's good enough for me," Heather replied as she crossed the room, getting underneath the makeshift blanket with Esmee, "As long as we don't get caught up here with our pants down."

Riley pressed the side of her face up against the frigid windowpane, squinting at the long stretch of wintry landscape leading back to the bridge.

Still no sign of the soldiers.

They were safe for now.

She stooped to unfurl the curtain over Esmee and Heather's faces, covering them from head to groin before sliding in on the other side. Both girls hugged the former nurse underneath the thick fabric, pooling their body heat together.

"How the hell are we gonna get all the way over to Utah?"

Heather murmured in the shadows, her striking green eyes still glittering in the gloom. "Even if we can kill whoever's coming after us, the soldiers are just gonna send more, until we end up like the rest of those people back at the school."

"We just have to keep moving," Riley replied, before an image of her family home in Redhurst flashed across her mind's eye. She refocused on Heather, "We can do this. If we can get far enough in front of them, I'll cover up our tracks and dig Dakota Fire Holes every time we need to make camp. The three of us can sleep in shifts. We'll pick up Taylor and the rest of your friends and keep on going – all the way to Cali. Putting two states in between us should throw the soldiers off our backs."

"Sounds like you've already given it some thought," Heather remarked, gazing back at her.

"I was making the trip with Keith and Jesse before we got captured," Riley began before stifling a smirk, deciding to sass the fiery redhead, "But I suppose I'll just have to make do with the two of you."

Heather snorted with a twitch of her eyebrows.

"You girls did a good job," Esmee said as she stirred in the stillness. She brought her hands to her face, breathing on her fingers and testing their dexterity. "Normally, I'd say we need to rest up until tomorrow – but if we rest now, we're dead. So, as soon as you two are up for it, we'll get dressed and start moving. We need to find something to wrap around our heads and necks before we go back out."

"I'm ready to go now," Heather's eyes met Riley's before turning to Esmee. "But just one thing before we do – after what I said about your friends back in the laneway, what made you decide to follow us?"

230

"I'll be honest," the woman sighed, tugging the top edge of their makeshift blanket down to stare up at the ceiling. "At first, I wanted to drown you both in the river. Then, I figured watching you and the soldiers kill each other before they came for me would be a lot easier. But now that you've saved my life... I'm thinking we might actually stand a chance of getting outta here if we work together."

Riley propped herself up on her elbow, narrowing her eyes at the former nurse, when her ears pricked up.

Somewhere in the distance, the sound of a snowmobile's engine whirred.

And another. And another.

CHAPTER 42

Riley and Heather hunkered down on either side of the hallway's front entrance, their misting breaths mingling over the invading snowdrift as they waited in anticipation.

Pulling the collar of her black skivvy up over her mouth, Riley locked eyes with Esmee standing by the staircase at the other end of the hall.

The former nurse's job was to distract whoever came in through the doorway, offering herself up as bait in a mock surrender, so that the other two could blindside their first victim.

Despite the apartment building having been picked clean, they had still managed to find a few items capable of doing some damage.

Riley's weapon of choice was the top of a toilet tank, while Heather was clutching a discarded phone charger in her good hand.

Esmee had sworn that she could find something better, until the fiery redhead explained that a few well-aimed thrusts from the two-pronged plug was more than enough to make a nice serve of eye socket soup.

Over the top of her pulse pounding in her eardrums, Riley could hear the snowmobiles singing in the distance as they navigated around the barricades on the bridge.

Roaring up the highway, the soldiers' engines soon rumbled to a stop outside the apartment building.

"Looks like they didn't get far," Sergeant Turnbull's deep voice floated through the open doorway as her heavy combat boots sank into the snow. "Knives out – I want this done quick and quiet."

"Quiet? No problem," Trask's surly voice came next, unsheathing his combat knife. "But does it have to be quick?"

"Just hang back and watch the windows," Corporal Newman grunted in exertion.

Riley's pupils dilated as a chunk of ice slid down the snowdrift into the hallway.

This is it, she gripped the edges of the toilet tank's lid in her gloved fingers.

Taking a galvanizing breath, she brought her weapon up over one shoulder, ready to swing, when the all too familiar sound of a snow shovel scraping and tossing reached her ears.

Newman was digging out the snowdrift blocking the entrance.

More chunks of ice rolled across the length of the hall, stopping at Esmee's feet.

The former nurse nodded at the two girls, confirming her confidence in the plan as she prepared to put on the show of their lives.

"You first," Heather mouthed at Riley, her green eyes laser-focused on the entrance.

"Wait!" Esmee shouted right on cue, her hands held up high.

A streak in the shadows flitted behind Esmee, and a flash of metal flew up to her neck.

"Newman, watch out!" Calvin warned the soldiers outside, holding a combat knife to Esmee's throat. He turned his piercing blue eyes on Riley and Heather, "Step out and drop your weapons, or she's dead."

"We're dead anyway!" Esmee reminded them, chin in the air. "Don't do it!!"

"You didn't think we'd just walk straight into a choke-point, did you?" Turnbull asked as she stepped into the hallway beside Calvin, the hulking sergeant holding her pistol on the pair of girls. "That might've worked for you back at the school – but you're dealing with us now. Toss the weapons."

"You're not gonna start shooting so close to the hotel," Riley called her bluff.

"What makes you so sure?" the oxlike officer cocked an eyebrow. "We already herded everyone back inside. Snow's coming down now too, that's another sound dampener. I could drop you both right now, and nobody would hear a thing."

"But why waste the ammo?" Trask lunged in through the front entrance, ramming his elbow into Riley's jaw, sending her staggering sideways into the wall.

Heather sprang on him from behind, but Newman caught her arm, twisting it behind her back until she dropped her two-pronged plug.

Riley snarled as Trask pressed the side of her face up against the wall, his free hand holding the cold edge of his combat knife to her throat.

Fuming resentfully, she let the toilet tank's top slip from her gloved fingers.

"Just the four of you, huh?" Heather glanced around the

room as the soldiers forced them down onto their knees. "Did you come to send us off? What a nice gesture."

"There used to be a time when we would've let you go," Turnbull holstered her pistol before ushering Calvin and Esmee towards the two girls. "Nowadays, we just execute you. Makes things less complicated."

"What's so complicated about letting us leave?" Esmee demanded, wrenching in Calvin's grip as he eased her down onto the floor.

"Can't have you rats running free," Trask growled, his breath hot in Riley's ear.

"Eventually, you'd set up your own community," Newman attempted to offer a better explanation. "If we let that go unchecked for too long, other survivors will start leaving for greener pastures. They're not greener though. They're all the same shade of shit. But it bleeds off our labor force, and we've got plenty of work around here that needs doing."

"That's why Drummond sent us to kill those people at the school," Riley supposed, the words sour in her mouth. She scowled up at Turnbull, "You lied to us, you fucking bitch. They weren't cannibals. They were innocent – they just didn't wanna be your slave labor anymore."

"You almost got it right," the hulking woman offered her a thin smile. "But Drummond never gave the order. The whole operation was my idea. That old man doesn't know half the shit that goes on – least of all, the threat that their community posed to our objective."

"And what objective is that?" Riley cocked her head to one side, feeling Trask's blade bite her skin. "You went AWOL from the rest of the army to help *save* civilians, remember? And you've ended up slaughtering them instead."

235

"Oh no, that wasn't me," Turnbull shared a grin with Trask and Newman before eyeing their prisoners again. "That was you and your friends. As far as I'm concerned, our hands are clean."

"You fucking used us, you butch piece of shit," Heather spat at the woman's feet.

"You're resources," Turnbull towered over Heather, "You were brought here to be used." Her smile faded as they heard another snowmobile roaring up the highway. "Newman, go see who that is."

"It's Rodriguez," he reported, peering out into the falling snow as the engine gave a few big revs before rumbling to a stop. "You sure took your time getting here."

"Leg day at the gym," the Latina soldier replied as she made her way inside, glancing at the three on their knees before looking up at Newman again. "You try walking through the snow while your thighs are on fire." She jerked her head towards Calvin, "What's the recruiter doing here?"

"Standing in for you," Trask grunted, glowering sidelong at her.

"I'll take it from here," Rodriguez said, offering to take the combat knife from Calvin.

"No!" he shouted suddenly, his blade still firmly pressed against Esmee's throat as he locked eyes with Turnbull. "I'm here. I'm doing this."

"That's the kind of attitude that's gonna win this war," the butch sergeant remarked, her stern gaze eyeing the three prisoners in turn. "Given the right motivation, assets like Fisher, the Bowmans, they'll do anything for us. That's why he's here."

"To do your dirty work?" Riley's voice dripped with scorn,

236

staring up at Calvin bitterly.

"To give one of you a second chance," he replied, his piercing blue eyes meeting hers. "I told you – I only need one more person for the month, and I'm set until spring. Turnbull agreed to let me try and convince you to stay. I'm the only chance you've got."

"Fuck you," she glared at him. The guy she'd known for years had become a complete stranger in her eyes. "I'm not going anywhere with you."

"You don't have to," Trask growled in her ear. "Go ahead, Fisher. Pick another."

"I should've left you to die on the side of that freeway," Esmee mumbled, her gaze downcast, with a single tear rolling down her cheek.

"Yeah, you should have," Calvin agreed, slashing the former nurse's throat.

CHAPTER 43

Riley stared down in horror as Esmee Gallagher's blood spread across the snow in the hallway, the former nurse gurgling and writhing on the floor.

After surviving for six months in the apocalypse, it wasn't the woman's sudden demise that shocked Riley so deeply – it was the ease of how casually Calvin could kill somebody who had saved his life.

Turnbull, Trask, Newman and Rodriguez idly watched as Calvin stepped over Esmee's body to face the other two on their knees.

He ran a thumb along his jaw line in contemplation.

"Changed your mind yet?" his piercing blue gaze lingered on Riley for a moment, before switching over to Heather. "Or maybe you'd be more appreciative of what's on offer. You look like you're a smart girl. You don't owe these two anything. How would you like to share my suite for the winter? Comes with all the perks – big bed, hot showers, plus any meds you might need."

Heather glanced sidelong at Riley, a guilty gaze in her green eyes.

"That last part," she began, cradling her swollen wrist with her good hand, "The doctor said I'd need four weeks rest, and a box of ibuprofen. Does that still stand if I'm in a suite?"

"Sure does," Calvin flashed his roguish grin at her in triumph. "Looks like we're gonna be spending a lot of time together."

"I guess that's it then," Trask supposed, pressing his combat knife against Riley's throat. Then, pausing for a moment, he asked, "You wanna do this one too?"

Calvin swallowed.

He glanced at Turnbull.

"That was the deal," the hulking sergeant reminded him. "Keep one. Kill two. Finish up, and you're all set."

He nodded in silence.

His gaze hardening, he turned towards Riley, fresh pearls of blood still dripping from his blade.

Trask withdrew his combat knife, the heavy-handed brute bearing down on Riley's shoulders instead, holding her in place.

"I'll make it quick," Calvin promised in a hollow voice, a shadow of his former self hiding behind a wet glimmer in his eyes.

"I won't," Riley's fists shook as she glowered up at him. "After I'm dead, I swear, you're gonna see me everywhere you go. When you walk down an empty corridor, you'll feel my cold breath on the back of your neck. When you take a hot shower, you'll hear my footsteps in the steam. When you lie down in that big bed of yours, you'll see me standing in the corner, watching you toss and turn all night long... You're not gonna make it to spring."

Heather snorted, gazing sidelong at her with a mixture of admiration and sorrow.

239

"I'll sleep well, knowing I gave you a chance," Calvin replied, taking a deep breath as he drew his arm back.

Riley refused to die on her knees though.

If I'm gonna die anyway, I may as well go down swinging.

His blade thrust towards her chest.

An icy surge of adrenaline bolted through her veins.

She slammed her forearm into his, blocking the blow as his strike fell short.

Grabbing his knife hand, she threw herself to the floor, escaping Trask's grip and twisting Calvin's wrist, the force so sudden that his tendons snapped.

"Shit!" Newman reached for his sidearm. "What's he –"

CRACK!

The corporal fell to the floor with a bullet hole in between his eyes.

"DON'T FUCKING MOVE!!" Keith Bowman's whiskey-cured voice barked across the hallway, swinging his pistol towards Trask next.

Sergeant Turnbull launched all of her hulking bodyweight at the former police officer, a stray shot going off as she tackled him through the drywall into an apartment behind the staircase.

"You brought him," Trask snarled at Rodriguez's empty holster. He whipped out his combat knife again as the two soldiers squared off against each other. "You just got Newman killed, you rat-simping whore."

Calvin was groaning in agony, cradling his broken wrist as he knelt beside Esmee's body, glancing up only to see Heather's sinister smile.

She grabbed a handful of his black hair before kneeing him in the face.

Riley searched the ground for his fallen knife, when Rodriguez fell to the floor in front of her, the Latina woman knocked unconscious.

"Let's hope you can last longer than her," Trask eyed Riley menacingly, ignoring Heather and Calvin's scuffle over Esmee's corpse. "It'll give me a good story to tell Wheeler when he wakes up."

Heart in her throat, unarmed against Trask's blade, Riley scrambled backwards towards the staircase, going for the high ground.

The iron-hearted brute marched after her with a surly grin, grabbing hold of her leg on the stairs and raising his combat knife.

Riley kicked out with her other boot, clocking him square in the face, but only knocking him back a step.

Spinning around, she scampered up the stairs, hearing his heavy footfalls hammering only a heartbeat behind.

She reached the top of the staircase, when Trask grabbed a handful of her thermal vest, wrenching her backwards.

Her heels hanging in the air, Riley caught hold of the railing, her gloved fingers frantically fumbling to find her zipper.

In the corner of her eye, she saw the gleaming edge of his blade thrusting towards her, and she cast caution to the wind.

Twisting around, she latched onto his knife arm and launched herself at Trask.

The pair tumbled down the stairs, wrestling for control of the weapon, limbs crashing hard on the steps until they landed in a tangled heap in the hallway.

Trask's combat knife was still clenched firmly in his hand, a serrated extension of his fist.

His other hand was reaching for his sidearm.

Pupils dilating, Riley flailed across the floor for something – *anything* – she could use.

Her gloved hand caught hold of an object – solid but small – Heather's phone charger.

Just as Trask's thumb flipped the safety lever off his pistol, she raised the two-pronged plug and rammed it into his eye socket, the surly soldier bellowing in pain as he fired blind slugs around the hallway.

Grabbing his gun hand was out of the question – his knife was still slashing at the air around him as he lurched to his feet.

Ducking and dodging the berserk barrage of bullets, Riley threw herself to the floor, hiding behind her discarded toilet tank's lid out of sheer desperation.

Trask showered the hallway with lead until his pistol clicked empty, and he glared around the room with his one good eye, balefully surveying the damage.

With a guttural roar, Riley surged to her feet and swung, the toilet tank's lid striking Trask full in the face, the phone charger exploding in his eye socket as his neck snapped sideways.

He fell backwards onto the staircase with his skull bent at an odd angle.

"You're food for the rats now, fucker," she panted, wiping her mouth.

Still breathing hard, she looked around the hallway to see Heather straddling Calvin's chest, his own combat knife clenched in her fist.

Both of them were struggling against each other with their one good hand.

A splotch of Esmee's blood dripped onto the base of Calvin's neck as he desperately tried to fend off the attack.

Riley fell to her knees beside them, watching as Heather leaned all of her weight into the downward thrust.

"Looks like you're spending the rest of your life with me, bitch," Heather growled over him, grunting in exertion.

"Help me, Riley," Calvin begged, the blade's tip licking at his throat. "It's me. It's still me. We were gonna go to the marina together, remember?"

"I remember," she grabbed Heather's hand. "You forgot."

Together, the two women plunged the knife into his throat, sinking the blade deep into his windpipe and slashing from left to right, crossing him the fuck out.

Riley and Heather locked eyes as Calvin Fisher drowned in his own blood beneath them.

"About before," Heather huffed, pulling the knife out to let his pulse pool onto the floor. "I want you to know, I planned on killing him in his sleep."

"How thoughtful of you," Riley gave her a small snort as she reached for Newman's sidearm. She jerked her head towards Rodriguez, "See if you can wake her up. I'll go check on Keith."

Flipping the pistol's safety lever off, Riley crept slowly towards the gaping hole in the drywall behind the staircase, only to see a shadowy pile of debris covered in dust.

Sidestepping through the open door, she aimed the barrel of her gun towards the unmistakable mass of Sergeant Turnbull's hulking body.

The oxlike officer was still moving underneath the wreckage, surrounded by chunks of drywall and broken planks from the kitchen cabinets that they had fallen through.

"Keith?" she asked in a small voice, glancing around the room. "Where'd you go?"

"Is that Riley?" he coughed in response, reaching his arm out from underneath the butch woman's body. "Get this fucking moose bitch off me!!"

CHAPTER 44

"Reminds me of being trapped under that bitch aunt of yours," Keith Bowman visibly shuddered as he recalled the trauma of Lake Springworth. He spat at Sergeant Turnbull's corpse, a steaming bullet hole in the side of her head. Brushing the dust off his fur-lined leather aviator jacket, he turned back to Riley, "You alright?"

"Yeah," her breath misted in the stillness, Newman's pistol rattling slightly in her hand. She flipped the safety lever on, before tucking it into the waistband of her ski pants at the small of her back. "You took your time with that shot."

"You try sneaking up on three soldiers," he chuckled as he moved to holster his sidearm, when he realized that he wasn't wearing a holster, and the gun wasn't his. He limped over to the door, "How is she?"

"She's fine," Rodriguez answered from the blood-covered floor in the hallway, gingerly touching the swelling in her jaw. The Latina soldier shook her head with a self-critical smile as she gazed at Trask's corpse on the staircase. "Bastard got me good though."

"What made you turn on your own people?" Heather asked

suspiciously, still clutching the combat knife in her good hand.

"Whoa, ease up," Keith took a few steps towards her, his pistol at the ready. "We just saved your ass."

"She barely even put up a fight," Heather cracked a cynical smile. She turned her attention back to the lone soldier. "Just because you *showed up*, don't think I've forgotten about the night you and your friends sent us to slaughter those people at the school."

"I was in the dark just as much as you," Rodriguez began as she slowly clambered to her feet, hands raised. "I heard the rumors about my squad, but I didn't wanna believe them. Even when shit didn't add up – like how Trask and Wheeler could never find the people who wanted to leave, but they could track down new survivors just fine." She looked down at the bodies of Corporal Newman, Calvin Fisher and Esmee Gallagher in turn. "But seeing the way they used Fisher against this poor woman... I'm sorry I didn't realize sooner."

"I told her what you told me about that pescatarian guy," Keith explained as he looked sidelong at Riley, his stony gaze blinking, finally having swallowed the hard truth. "That's why she agreed to help me when..." he snorted, his somber face cracking into a grin, "When we heard three crazy bitches jumped into the fucking river."

"Who else but me, right?" Riley rubbed the back of her neck, sharing his smile.

"Here," Rodriguez tossed her the keys to their snowmobile.

Heather finally lowered her knife, but not her guard.

"We got Jesse to fill it all the way up," Keith explained, before patting down the dead soldiers for their water canteens and any extra ammo. "There's a couple cans of gas in the back too. You're gonna need it if you're gonna make it all the way down to Whistler's Valley."

"I'm not going to Texas," Riley replied, her gaze switching between him and Rodriguez. "You should come with us. They're either gonna kill you or kick you out when they find out what happened here."

"I'm not leaving Jesse behind," Keith shook his head, offering her the spare magazines and the water canteens. "I don't wanna go back out there anyway – living one day at a time, not knowing if we'll have anything to eat tomorrow."

"We aren't all like Turnbull," Rodriguez reassured them, twisting her lips as she realized she was walking the line between helping and recruiting. "Captain Drummond is a reasonable man. He'll listen to our story. You two don't have to go anywhere."

"I'd rather shit in my hands and clap," Heather snorted as the four of them trudged back out into the snow.

"I'm gonna take my chances here with Drummond," Keith said as he climbed onto one of the fallen soldiers' snowmobiles. He turned in his seat to look back at Riley, "You can stay or go. I'm not gonna stop you."

"Whatever you decide," Rodriguez added as she mounted up, "Just know that we won't be able to get you this much gas a second time. Jesse only got away with it because we said it was an emergency."

"If you're staying, then give me the keys," Heather locked eyes with Riley as frosty flakes fell around them. "I'm still going after my sister, with or without you."

Riley clutched the keys in her gloved hand.

She blew a long plume of mist as she studied the resolve on Heather's face. The pair of sisters wouldn't have been split up in the first place if it hadn't been for Riley and her friends raiding their supplies.

And staying at the hotel wasn't going to get her any closer to Redhurst.

We can't change the shit that we're sinking in, she thought to herself. *But when somebody tosses you a line, you'd be stupid not to pull yourself out.*

"Thanks for everything, Keith," Riley finally broke her silence, heading towards the one snowmobile that didn't have any keys in the engine. "Could you tell Jesse…" she faltered for a moment, biting her bottom lip. "Tell him I'll see him again one day."

Sucking his front teeth in silence, Keith stared up at the snow falling from the gray clouds in the sky, the snowflakes settling onto the bloodstained shoulders of his fur-lined leather aviator jacket.

It wasn't the answer that he had wanted to hear, but he nodded all the same.

"Be careful out there," he held her gaze for a long time before turning his keys, the snowmobile's engine roaring to life.

Riley brushed her face as she watched Keith and Rodriguez speeding back towards the bridge, the military blockade barely visible beyond the curtain of falling snow.

She knew that it was going to be tough – surviving on the road again – but she could handle tough.

She was built for tough.

"Come on, let's saddle up," Heather said as she climbed onto the snowmobile, scooting back for Riley to take the reins. "We better get back on the road before it gets any worse out here."

"Yeah," Riley agreed, straddling the seat and pushing the keys into the ignition. "Do you mind if we take the long way over to Utah? I need to stop by my dad's grave first."

* * *

Keep reading to receive an email when the next book gets published!

Find out what happens next!

Thank you so much for reading Scavengers of The Fall. I hope you enjoyed the story.

Join my newsletter here to receive an email when the next book gets published!
www.steveheuzinkveld.com/newsletter

I'd also like to invite you to my Book Lovers Facebook Group. Chat with me, have a character named after you, talk with other fans, and win exclusive prizes and giveaways.
Join the fun!
www.facebook.com/groups/SteveHeuzinkveldVIPFans

Here's a QR code so you don't have to type out any links:

ACKNOWLEDGMENTS

As always, first and foremost, I want to thank my beautiful wife, Hariezoy, for supporting me and encouraging me every single day, and for giving me the freedom to burn the midnight oil to hit the keyboard every night until the sun comes up.

A huge thanks also goes to my Patreon followers, Greg Hyndman, Rupert Lugo and Martin Georgiev. Your continued support has really helped soften the financial impact in hiring professional artists for my book covers, the ongoing website costs, and all of the other expenses that it takes to keep this author's dreams alive!

I want to thank the admins and moderators of all my favorite Facebook groups as well – you volunteer so much of your time to keeping the post-apoc genre at the forefront of my news feed. A special thanks goes to Josh Atkinson, Laura Daleo, Bill Kennedy, Jeff Pelletier and Sylvester Barzey for letting me spread the word about my books. And an honorable mention goes to the people behind Books of Horror as well, because their reader community rocks!

And of course, my heartfelt thanks goes to Ana Schaeffer for introducing me to all of the amazing Facebook groups out there. Your feedback and guidance during my early days of writing in this genre planted a seed for this story, and I hope you've enjoyed reading it as much as I've enjoyed writing it!

And last but not least, thank you. As an independently-published author, this is very often a one-man show, and after the hours upon hours I've invested into this project, it means the world to me that you've taken the time to meet the characters living in my head.

I'd love to put your name here in my future books, right alongside Greg, Rupert and Martin. Join us on Patreon for access to never-before-seen chapters from my other works, as well as autographed copies of future books, all while helping me to bring more stories to life!

www.patreon.com/SteveHeuzinkveld

P.S. I love hearing from my fans - feel free to contact me any time!

-Steve
author@SteveHeuzinkveld.com
www.SteveHeuzinkveld.com

.